THE PROMISE

PROMISE

OF THE WILLOWS

A NOVEL

THE PROMISE OF THE WILLOWS

A NOVEL

JEAN GRANT

THOMAS NELSON PUBLISHERS
Nashville • Atlanta • London • Vancouver

APR 9 6

Copyright © 1994 by Jean Grant

Published in Nashville, Tennessee, by Thomas Nelson, Inc., Publishers, and distributed in Canada by Word Communications, Ltd., Richmond, British Columbia, and in the United Kingdom by Word (UK), Ltd., Milton Keynes, England.

Scripture quotations are from the NEW KING JAMES VERSION of the Bible. Copyright © 1979, 1980, 1982, Thomas Nelson, Inc., Publishers.

Library of Congress Cataloging-in-Publication Data

Grant, Jean.
  The promise of the willows : a novel / Jean Grant.
    p. cm. — (The Salinas Valley saga)
    ISBN 0-7852-8102-9 (pb)
    1. Christian communities—Salvation Army—History—Fiction.
2. Community life—California—Fort Romie—Fiction.   3. Farm life—California—Fort Romie—Fiction.   4. Family—California—Fort Romie—Fiction.   5. Fort Romie (Calif.)—Fiction.   I. Title.
II. Series.
PS3557.R2663P76   1994
813'.54—dc20   93-45260
                                         CIP

Printed in the United States of America
4 5 6 7 - 00 99 98 97 96 95

"The Landless Man to the Manless Land"

In the spring of 1898, the Salvation Army purchased 520 acres four miles from the town of Soledad, California, in the Salinas Valley. Their goal, according to Commissioner Frederick Booth-Tucker, was this: "Place the waste labor on the waste land by means of waste capital, and thereby convert this trinity of modern waste into a trinity of production."

About twenty city families came to the colony, called Fort Romie, in the fall of 1898. By 1901, only one of the original families remained, and the land was resold, mostly to people with farming experience.

That much is fact, and the good land and the hard life and the faith of the farmers are fact. The people and the incidents in The Promise of the Willows *are fictional.*

Chapter One

*C*arrie McLean stood among
the motley cluster of anx-
ious men, fidgety wives, and excited children on the
bare, wooden railway station platform. The train had
dropped the twenty families who would be remembered
in Salinas Valley history as the Fort Romie Colony in
front of a tiny frame depot. Its single coat of yellow paint
was peeling.

Covering the 150 miles from San Francisco had been
an all-day trip in the dry September heat. Carrie, like the
others, was accustomed to the cool, foggy climate of the
San Francisco Peninsula, and September, the warmest
time of the year, was not her favorite month. It had been
bright and clear when they'd left at dawn, and the farther
south they had gone the more relentless had been the
glaring sun and blistering east wind. The milk bottles she
had filled with water and carried in her carpetbag had
been empty by noon, shared with the thirsty children
whose mothers had been less well-prepared.

Carrie fanned herself listlessly as she surveyed the little country town that was to be her new home. Though she'd never been beyond the outskirts of San Francisco before, like all San Franciscans she knew the city was the best place in the whole world. But Papa had decided to move his family to this place called Soledad. Papa was sure things would be better here.

The slender eighteen year old's deep-set brown eyes peered from under the sunbonnet that protected her fair skin. From the station platform she could see nearly the whole village of Soledad. There was only one street, a dusty trail along the railroad. She sighed as she read the wooden signpost which leaned, as everything in town seemed to, to the southeast. "Front Street! That's a laugh. What does it think it's in front of? It's no wider than the trolley tracks down the middle of Market Street."

A few unpainted sheds and one or two false-fronted shops straggled along Front Street. An emporium, even. As Carrie noted the familiar name on the shabby shop she recalled the time she'd spent in the "real" Emporium. Ten hours a day, six days a week for the past two years, she had sold ladies' gloves under its massive dome. Her legs ached just to think of it. At least she was free of that now.

"Ain't it peaceful, Carrie? Peaceful and quiet and clean."

Carrie glanced toward her father as he spoke.

Sam McLean stood at the end of the platform, arms outstretched as if to embrace the entire valley. "Oh, Carrie, think of living here, waking up every morning to the sight of those golden hills and the line of willow trees

2

along the river. And soon there will be green fields—our fields, Carrie."

But Carrie, who had known nothing but the bustle of the San Francisco of the gay nineties, gazed silently at the tiny village. Two or three dozen houses were scattered along a few paths to the east. One church spire peeped over the so-called business section. Down at the end of the street she saw a one-room schoolhouse. That was it, all of it. *At least the place is well named,* she thought. *Soledad. Solitude.*

The blazing September sun burned down on the group as they waited at the depot. Carrie was sticky with perspiration. The wind blew steadily up the valley and stirred soil from the few plowed fields into swirls of black dust that clung to her wet face. As she wiped the moisture from her forehead, her handkerchief was muddied by the grime. "And Papa talks about how clean it is here." She chuckled ruefully.

A Salvation Army officer clattered up in an open hay wagon. His team looked as forlorn and tired as the colonists. "I'm Captain John Stoneham. Sorry to be so late," he apologized, with an offhanded shrug. "Been down at the lumberyard. I've got good news, though. There was some mix-up, but the wood for the cabins is finally here."

"Wood for cabins?" The waiting pioneers murmured anxiously. "We thought each plot had a cabin. Where are the farms we were promised?"

The man held his hands aloft as if he were preaching. "Comfort, now. There is no real problem. The land is there to the west, along the line of the hills, and it is good

3

land too. We'd hoped to have the cabins built, but the Lord did not will it so."

"But what are we to do? We have left our homes. Where shall we sleep?"

The captain's thin lips turned up in what passed for a smile. "It has all been arranged. The women and children will stay at a local inn, Los Coches, while the men build the cabins."

The colonists milled about briefly, chattering.

"The Murphys, Bowens, and Phillips are going back to the city, Papa," Carrie reported. "Perhaps we should go too."

"Now, Carrie, it's just a little setback. I have three strong sons to help with our cottage. It will be built before you know it. I've dreamed of this day all my life—the day I'd have my own farm. My only regret is that your mother did not live to see it."

Rob, the eldest McLean son, went with Sam and the other men to inspect the homesites. Captain Stoneham left the women and children at the inn in the care of two Salvation Army lassies, Sister Addie Warren and Lieutenant Margaret Andrews.

Los Coches was an old ranch house from the Mexican era. Like everything else in Soledad, it was dusty, but inside its foot-thick adobe walls it was surprisingly cool. Carrie gratefully settled her younger brothers, Will and Tim, into their room.

"When can I plant my seeds, Carrie?" Will asked.

"You could start a small vegetable garden on the back of your neck." Carrie laughed as she scrubbed the topsoil from behind his ears. "I don't think this is the time of year to plant seeds, Will. First, we must build our house and plow. Then after the rains come, we will plant our seed."

"Me too. I can help too. Papa said so."

"Certainly you can, Tim. We will need all the hands we can find, I expect."

"Papa says fresh corn that you pick yourself is sweet as candy. When will we have some, Carrie?"

How could she explain this new farming life to eight- and ten-year-old city boys? "It takes a long time for crops to grow. Not days or weeks. It will be almost this time next year before we harvest our first crops."

"I get my chickens right away, though, Carrie. You promised." Tim interrupted, so eager to start a life he knew nothing about. "You promised I could take care of the chickens."

Carrie thought of the tiny bag of silver pieces she'd tucked into her corset cover. She wondered how many of them it would take to buy chickens. "Soon, Tim. As soon as the house is finished we will build a pen and find some chickens. Then you can feed them and gather the eggs."

Sam had filled his young sons with such excitement at the idea of being farmers at last, but Carrie had her doubts. *If this is such rich land as the Salvation Army people told us, why is all the land along the road we traveled empty and brown?* she wondered.

Captain Stoneham preached that evening at the Los Coches, as he did every evening and twice on Sunday. Carrie assumed that was part of the price the would-be farmers had to pay for their farms. That first night he talked of Commissioner Booth-Tucker's dream of "The Landless Man to the Manless Land."

That was what had brought the McLeans and their companions to Soledad. In 1898, America's cities were crowded with unemployed men. The financial panic had hit San Francisco especially hard, and Sam McLean was one of many who, discouraged and unable to support their families, had turned from despair to drink.

The Salvation Army preached on street corners, and their message started with personal salvation, which had reached Sam and restored his hope. But the work of the Army wasn't all spiritual. The dream of its founder and his followers was to show Jesus' love by helping their fellow men—feeding the hungry, healing the sick, and putting the down-and-out back on their feet.

Papa always wanted a farm anyhow, Carrie thought. When he had heard of the Salvation Army's plan to settle a group of poor families on land it would sell to them on easy credit, he'd been one of the first to sign up.

The only farms Carrie had ever seen before that morning were the small truck farms and dairies that clustered at the south edge of San Francisco, watered by the virtually constant morning fogs. The sheer vastness of the Salinas Valley overwhelmed her. *What will happen to us all?* she wondered. *How will we learn how to make things grow? Where will the money come from to live on until there are crops, and how will we make the annual payments on the land itself?*

Carrie was an old eighteen. She'd been mother to her younger brothers for the past six years, but she felt very young herself that evening. She forced herself to set aside her doubts by concentrating on her immediate surroundings. She tried to listen to Captain Stoneham's sermon, but she was a well-bred young lady, and his call to sinners to repent had little meaning for her. Of what did she need to repent?

Instead, she found herself studying the captain. *He's a cool, spare man,* she thought, *too thin, like me, and with dull brown coloring like the dust of the valley. He's young, though, too young both to be so somber and to be a Salvation Army officer.*

The captain led the singing as Miss Addie jangled her tambourine and Lieutenant Margaret played her cornet. *How could they have so much energy?* Carrie wondered. She was exhausted from the journey. As she drowsed she recalled the sonorous organ and the gentle comfort of the preaching at her mother's church. It had been years since Mama had taken her there, back before Timmy was born and Liz McLean's health failed. The Jesus Carrie came to know there had been gentle too.

The Savior the Salvationists preach seems hardly a Prince of Peace, she reflected. *But how can I complain, when Papa has quit drinking and all my brothers have been saved? Before she died, Mama had thanked God for the Army, though she never could abide their methods.*

The service was disrupted by the arrival of a half dozen men of the area, who came to quench their thirst at the Los Conches bar. They were ranch hands, and Carrie assumed that they were regulars there. Though they did not come to the service, they sang their rowdy songs just across the hall and blocked the way as the colonists went to their rooms afterward.

"Come to save the cowboys, lassie?"

"Where's the brass band, preacher?"

"Gonna convert the jackrabbits?"

"Too late to save us from hell, brother. We're already there."

As Carrie reached the foot of the stairs she felt a rough hand on her arm. "And where's your Army bonnet, pretty lassie? Or ain't you enlisted yet?"

He was a broad-shouldered, stocky man with hair as red as her father's used to be, Carrie noticed. Long copper mustaches drooped around his firm chin. His teasing smile showed even, white teeth, and his skin was fair, though freckled from many hours working in the hot sun and fierce wind.

His breath was foul with the rum he'd been drinking, and his voice was rude. He had the nerve to turn Carrie's face toward him and look straight into her eyes, and she felt as if his cool, blue stare peered into her very soul. Yet his impertinent touch was surprisingly gentle.

"They call me Matt, Matt Hanlon."

Chapter Two

*T*he next morning a cool fog settled the black dust and calmed Carrie's fears. She had offered to go along and help Lieutenant Margaret register the colony's children at the town school. They left the children there and stopped at the railway station for some building supplies that had arrived from Oakland. Carrie was grateful for the opportunity to talk to Lieutenant Margaret about the valley as they drove back. "Twenty-two more children. It will be a veritable flood. I hope they have desks enough," Carrie said.

"Don't let the size of the town fool you, Carrie. There are lots of people back in the hills."

"Why are they in the hills? Why don't they farm the flats? Wouldn't that be easier?"

"Seems so, but I don't know that much about farming or about the land for that matter. I'm told the flats flood in winter, though it certainly doesn't look like it now."

"The man we talked to in San Francisco said there was a river. Is it on the other side of the town?"

Margaret laughed then. "This is it. We're crossing it now."

Carrie looked to either side of the road. Ragtag lines of willow trees wandered to the north and south, and scattered clumps of grass clung to the fringes of tiny mud holes.

"This is the Salinas River? But then there is land right here, along it, going to waste while farmers struggle on the high ground. I don't understand."

"It's a California river, and this is autumn. Come the winter rains, we will have to ferry the children to school by raft."

"You seem to know quite a bit about it. Have you been here long?"

"Oh my, no. Addie and I came down about two weeks ago to help Captain Stoneham find a place for all of you to stay temporarily. But we've been talking to the girls at the inn and to the farmhands who come there. We tell them about the Lord, and they tell us about Soledad. The captain's been here for several months. He was part of the committee that selected the site."

"How did they choose it? It seems so desolate."

"Mostly, it was cheap," Margaret admitted. "Mr. Romie bought it at a foreclosure sale and was persuaded that it would be a charitable thing to make it available for Commissioner Booth-Tucker's experiment."

"Besides," Carrie snorted, "it obviously wasn't worth anything to him."

"It's not bad land, Carrie. It's just been a dry year," Lieutenant Margaret explained. "Did you know it was a Catholic mission a generation or two ago?"

"Yes. Papa said that meant it had been farmed, so it could be again. There are even irrigation ditches to bring the river water to it and some old fruit trees. Papa hoped there would be trees on our plot."

"Most of you people are like me. Wouldn't know a fruit tree from chaparral," observed Margaret. "Captain Stoneham said your father was different. Did he have a farm once?"

"No, not Papa. His father had a farm, the best farm in Illinois, he used to tell Papa. He sold it to come to the gold fields in the fifties, when Papa was a baby. Then his wife died at the mines, and he and my papa wandered from one camp to another until Papa was old enough to get work in the city. But his father never forgot the land, and Papa has always dreamed of it.

"Papa's always had lots of dreams." Carrie paused, remembering how often her father's dreams had failed them in the past. "But mostly he dreams about having his own land. That's why we've come. Papa says God has answered all his prayers now. His sons will have land, and his daughter won't waste away in a city shop."

"You sound a little uncertain. I know it's a new life and it's hard, but how do you feel about being here?" asked Margaret.

Carrie shrugged. "I haven't really thought about how I feel. I had no choice. Since Mother died there is no one else to look after my little brothers. And working in the shop was very hard, of course. So many demanding customers and the manager always onto us for every little thing. 'Be polite. Smile. Handle the goods carefully, girls. The customer is always right.' Yes, I guess I'm glad to be away from that, but . . ." She squared her shoulders and lifted her chin. "But I've learned not to get my hopes up too much. You just get hurt that much more."

Lieutenant Margaret looked at the girl beside her. Carrie carried herself proudly and she sounded so self-assured, but her long lashes were wet with the tears she was too proud to shed. Margaret urged the horses on.

It was noontime and the wind had driven off the fog. The hot sun and swirls of black dust had returned when Carrie and Lieutenant Margaret pulled the wagon up to the tent the men had pitched as temporary Army head-quarters. They opened the lunch baskets they had brought, and the men laid aside their tools.

As they bowed their heads in prayer, a few ranch hands rode past. "Pray hard," they called out. "You'll need the help of the Almighty if you intend to farm the Salinas."

Carrie thought she recognized one of the rough voices. It was that redhead, Matt Hanlon.

The blistering hot wind blew nearly every day through the rest of September and most of October. The hills faded from dry gold to an exhausted brown. There had been so little rain in the last year that cattle on the driest ranges were already starving to death. The people of the valley prayed, and the Fort Romie colonists joined them in praying for early rain. Still, the colonists were selfishly grateful that it did not come before they moved into their new cabins.

"That's the last of the packing crates, Carrie." Sam set the sturdy box on the plank-topped sawhorses they were using as a kitchen table. "I'm off to plow the west field. I have use of the team for the whole day, and if we are to have crops next summer, I must sow now before the rains come."

They had only a few boxes to unpack. *I guess that is a good thing about being poor,* Carrie thought. The last box was special. She began to remove the bright blue and white plates from the shredded newspaper. Mama's prized china, her wedding present from her parents. She'd had so few pretty things. How she had treasured it.

Carrie stacked the fragile plates and bowls next to the graniteware dishpan. As she filled the pan with hot water from the teakettle on the wood stove, she wished once again that Mama could be here. Carrie remembered her mother's wispy figure bending over the sink in their dingy flat.

"Yes, Carrie, a house all to ourselves. Oh, not on Nob Hill, of course. My family wasn't rich, but we did have a hired girl to help with the housework. Father was a teamster. He had three teams and drivers working for him. That's how I met Papa, in fact."

"Tell me how it was, Mama. What was Papa like when you were young?"

"Ah, when we were young." Liz's eyes would mist then, and she would draw a chapped hand across her brow, brushing back the salt-and-pepper curls that escaped her prim chignon. "Papa was a big man, broad-

13

shouldered and strong. His hair was copper bright, brighter than Robbie's even."

"Why did I have to be the one with the mousy brown stuff?"

Her mother didn't seem to hear her. "Sam never yelled at the horses the way the other drivers did. All he had to do was say whoa in that firm, calm way he had, and they just knew he was in charge."

Carrie knew the story by heart. "And when he said, 'Marry me, Liz,' you knew it too."

"Something like that, I guess, Carrie. Oh, he courted me like a real gentleman, for all he'd been brought up in the gold fields." Then her mother's voice would lose the lilt that had crept in momentarily. She would continue flatly, in time to the swish of the dishrag. "He told me about his plans. He was saving his money for his own team. Then, when he had his own business, he'd buy a little farm across the Bay or an orchard down around Santa Clara, and he'd haul his own produce, and his neighbors', too, and sell it in the city. His plans—"

The bitterness would come into her mother's voice. "His plans. His dreams. You can't eat dreams, Carrie, and you can't feed them to hungry children. Don't ever marry a man who dreams."

Maybe Papa's still dreaming, Carrie thought as she stacked the bright plates on the newsprint-covered shelves. She looked around the bare room.

The plank walls were unpainted. Four straight-backed oak chairs stood around the makeshift table, and a pair of scratched rockers shared the faded rag rug from their city

14

flat. In the corner beyond the big iron stove was a narrow iron bedstead, Carrie's bed.

The beds? Carrie's mind came back to the present with a sudden jolt. The next thing she had to do was make up the two big beds in the other room for Sam and the boys. "We'll all be too exhausted after supper to make them," she said.

As she gave the last pillow a final fluff, Carrie heard the whinny of a horse and looked out the window, surprised that Papa was back so soon from plowing. *Oh no! Company! Not on our first day!*

The two women drove a fine buckboard, which looked nearly new despite its coat of valley dust. As the younger woman helped the elder down, Carrie noticed their old-fashioned but neat calico gowns and sunbonnets.

"Hello, there. I'm Anna Arnesen." The tall, broad-browed blonde spoke with a hint of an accent.

Scandinavian, Carrie thought.

"And this is Britta Svensen." The gray-haired woman smiled shyly, as Mrs. Arnesen continued. "We dry-farm over across the river. My Harold told me you folks were moving in today, and I said to Britta, 'Britta, we must drive over and welcome that family.'"

Carrie felt a moment of panic. Her apron was still splotched from the dishwashing, limp locks drooped from her pompadour, and she had nothing on the kitchen shelf to accompany a hospitable cup of tea.

But Anna chattered on, as she reached for a basket in the buckboard. "You'll not have the time for baking for a day or two," she explained, uncovering two crusty loaves of bread and a small crock. "I hope you like wild black-berry preserves."

"Won't you come in?" Carrie stammered. "I wasn't expecting guests, but . . ."

"We're not guests. We're neighbors." A firm nod punctuated her words, and Carrie knew the question was settled.

Mrs. Svensen had lifted a basket from the buckboard, too, and her blue eyes sparkled as she opened it to reveal a very unhappy looking hen. "Mrs. Svensen doesn't speak much English," Anna explained. "But she has brought you a setting hen to help you get started."

"Oh, thank you so much. My brother Tim has been promised he can have some chickens. He's already built a pen for them. He's only eight years old, though, and I'm afraid none of us knows much about chickens."

"There isn't much to know. These babies will hatch in about a week, and Mama Hen will take good care of them. But Tim goes to school with my boy, Eric. Eric will tell him what he needs to know. You'll have a good laying flock before you know it."

Anna's optimism was contagious. "I'm sure we will, Mrs. Arnesen. And later, when we get settled, we will repay your kindness."

"Here, we all try to help each other, Carrie. It is my Harold's team that your father borrowed. That's how we knew you were moving in today. When Harold said you were city people and no mama to tend the house and youngsters, well, I said to Britta, 'We're going over and let that girl know we're around to help.'"

16

"I just don't know how to tell you how much I appreciate your kindness." Carrie was surprised to hear her usually reserved self rattle on. "I was feeling so alone and, well, a little afraid this morning. I have so much to learn. Thank you for coming."

She hesitated, wanting to offer them something in return. "Would you like a cup of tea?" she asked. "I know it's terribly hot, but we've no ice, and the water is hauled from the river so it is warm too."

"Cool water is a luxury to all of us this year. Most of the wells have been dry for months." For the first time Anna's smile faded. "We all carry water in drums from the river. There has been no rain since last March and precious little before that."

"Then how do you grow crops?" asked Carrie.

"There are methods for making use of the moisture from the dew and fogs. We grow barley, which requires little. Even so, our harvest was half as much this year as usual."

"But we've counted on being able to grow our own food—vegetables, grain for chickens, hay for a cow," Carrie cried.

"The hay is hard. The pastures produce so little. But for vegetables we use what we carry in the drums. First, you wash yourself, then your clothes, and then you pour it on the garden."

"But the soap?"

"No harm. Some say it is good; it kills the bugs. Maybe it does. At least it is water. Have you started a vegetable garden yet?"

17

"Now? Don't I have to wait until spring to plant vegetables?"

"Oh, heavens no, Carrie. Plant the root crops now and cabbage too. Water them with the wash water, like I said, until it rains. They'll come along, bit by bit, and then when spring comes they'll shoot up and you'll have carrots and turnips and beets before you can imagine. Do you have seed?"

"I have a little money set aside. What should I buy now? You said carrots and turnips. Cabbage?"

"No need to spend your savings, Carrie. You'll need that for other things. I've lots of seed saved from this year's harvest. I'll send some by Eric and your brothers tomorrow. I'll send a few sweet green peas too. They will not grow in the summer heat, but in the winter, in a sheltered spot they will thrive."

Carrie tried to protest, but it seemed that what Anna decided, Anna did. "Well, if you are sure you have extra."

"Plenty and more. Now, Carrie, we know you've lots to do, and I'm sure you're already tuckered out. So we're going to go on and visit the Andersens, up the road. I wonder if they're Danes, like us. Do you happen to know? Maybe I won't have to do all the talking, if they are."

Carrie didn't know. But she suspected even if they did speak Danish, Britta would still have trouble getting a word in edgewise.

As the buckboard rolled off toward the Andersens' cabin, Carrie realized that her father and the boys would soon be back. She suddenly found she was not so lonely. Humming to herself, Carrie pared vegetables for supper.

Sam wiped his soup bowl nearly clean with the heel of Anna's loaf of bread. "That was a mighty good meal, daughter. I'm surprised you used your mother's willow-ware, though. You know she intended you to have it when you marry, and you have always said you don't want it broken."

"When I marry might be a while, Papa, and I thought this was a special occasion."

"Right you are, Carrie. It is a very special occasion. Now, boys, scrub that good country dirt off your hands and faces, and be quick about it. We're off to thank the Lord for his blessings, and I don't want to be late for the captain's opening prayer."

Sam dressed in his Army uniform of course, though Carrie had not had time to press it. Not having become a member herself, Carrie shook the worst wrinkles from her dark green skirt and a gingham shirtwaist. *Maybe I should sell one or two of my best dresses,* she thought, *since the things I had to buy for work at the Emporium are not suitable for the country.* Despite Anna's encouragement, she knew there would be no harvest—and no money—for several months. No one seemed to think of that—none of the Fort Romie group at any rate.

The captain prayed most determinedly for the lost that night, and the testimonies were full of praise for the Lord's goodness. While Carrie thanked the Lord for sending Anna and Britta to her, her prayers were for rain and for paying work while they awaited the harvest.

After the meeting, Captain Stoneham made a point of speaking to Sam and Carrie. "You seem very cheerful this evening, Miss Carrie."

19

"It is good to be settled in, Captain."

"And just how does your new home suit you, now that you are living in it?"

"Oh, very well. I cannot remember ever being where it was so clean or so quiet. I find myself stopping every so often just to listen. No shouting from the flat above or rattling of wagons and hooves on the street."

"Do you miss the sounds of the city, Miss Carrie?"

"A trifle, perhaps." She laughed a little, remembering other noises. "But I don't think I shall ever miss the noises of the shop—the whining and complaining and demanding. I certainly hope I never have to go back to that."

"Yes, Miss Carrie, this is a much better life, and we are especially happy to have you here among us. I've been told by Lieutenant Margaret that you've been most helpful to some of the ladies in caring for their babies while they did their unpacking. I wanted to give you my thanks for your assistance."

"Oh, that was nothing, Captain. I wasn't that busy while we were at the inn, and I like children," she said modestly.

He smiled then, and Carrie was surprised to realize she was comparing his kindly look with Matt Hanlon's cool, mocking stare.

Chapter Three

*P*apa had invited Captain Stoneham to share a Sunday dinner not long after the McLeans moved into their cabin, and Carrie painstakingly prepared the best meal she could with their limited funds.

"A most excellent dinner, Miss Carrie," the captain said, as he laid down his fork. "I thank you and your father for your hospitality."

"Thank you, Captain Stoneham." Carrie left the table to serve the apple pie she had baked.

"We're pleased you could share the Lord's provision with us." Sam winked at Carrie. "You have to admit, daughter, that rabbits did not walk up to our doorstep in the city."

He was right about that, Carrie admitted to herself. Though there would be no crops for months, Eric Arnesen had taught Will how to set rabbit traps, and now they had fresh meat every few days at no cost.

"The Lord is blessing our labors, Sam," the captain said. "I noticed your wheat has already sprouted with the early rains."

"I've potatoes set too," Sam answered proudly, "and Carrie's kitchen garden will give us cabbages and carrots for our rabbit stews long before summer."

"So you are becoming a farmer, too, Miss Carrie?"

"Yes, Captain Stoneham. I don't know much about it," she admitted, "but when Mrs. Arnesen and her friend called to welcome us, they told me when and how to plant and shared their seed with me."

"How do you get enough water?" the captain inquired. "Most of our families can scarcely do the cooking and cleaning with their ration from the colony's well."

"Oh, I dumped the wash water on the garden, and had some left over for the apple trees, until the Lord answered our prayers with the abundant rainfall these past weeks."

"Abundant is right," Rob growled. "One day the world is brown dust, and the next day we're in muck up to our boot tops."

"We had to take a raft across the river to school four times. It was fun."

"Fun for you, Will. Not for the ones rowing the rafts."

"Now, Robbie." Sam's voice lost some of its lilt as he turned to his oldest son. "You should be proud to be trusted to take the children across the river. And the rains are a great blessing. We couldn't survive without them. Seeing that river running full and wide should bring joy to us all.

"Carrie, that smells wonderful!" Sam continued, as Carrie sliced the warm pie she'd just taken from the oven.

"Isn't she a wonder, Captain? The apples on those old trees are just about all wizened up, but she takes them and makes a pie that smells like ambrosia."

"Rabbit with dumplings and apple pie." Captain Stoneham rubbed his hands together in anticipation as Carrie served the juicy slices. "Sam, I have not had a feast like this since I left my dear mother's roof."

"The Army doesn't provide people with many luxuries, I'd guess," Rob said.

"That's for certain. The Lord sends enough for our needs always, but it takes a woman's touch, I do believe, to turn enough into a feast."

"What you need, Captain, is a good wife," Sam said. Carrie flushed, wishing her father would at least be a little more subtle.

"Well, Sam, you may be right, but as yet the Lord has not sent the proper woman across my path. We may only marry other officers, you know, and only with official permission."

"You could marry Lieutenant Margaret," Will piped in.

"Hush, Will. You shouldn't say such things to your elders." Carrie glared at her brother and then answered his query. "Lieutenant Margaret told me she is engaged already. She was assigned here for the required period of separation, to test their commitment to each other. But she expects to be married soon."

"Another piece, Captain?" Sam offered. "Sure is good pie."

Carrie felt the color rise in her cheeks again as she realized her father had turned the conversation back to her cooking. "Excuse me, please. I must get water to clean up the dishes."

The captain left soon to prepare for the afternoon's street preaching in Soledad. Rob disappeared, off to meet his new friends in town. The little boys went out to check Will's traps before the evening preaching.

Carrie pulled one of the rockers close to the stove, for the November rain was a cold one, and she opened her mother's old mending basket.

Sam settled into the opposite rocker and began, "Carrie, there are times when I sorely miss your mother."

She knew what was coming. It was her father's inevitable opening for a fatherly lecture.

"It's hard for a father to talk about such things to his daughter, Carrie, but you are of an age to be thinking about marriage."

"Yes, Papa, or about not marrying."

"Nonsense. Every girl wants, and needs, a husband. Otherwise—"

"Otherwise nothing, Papa. These days a girl can do lots of other things. I could support myself. I shall, when Tim and Will are older and you don't need me here."

"Will you go back to the city and back to the shop? Carrie, I'll not see you sent to an early grave by such work, nor will I see you in service either!"

"I've thought about a school, Papa. I could learn typewriting, maybe, or telegraphy or the telephone switchboard."

"And look forward to a lonely old age without husband or children."

24

"I'm not going to marry just anyone, Papa. I will not marry just to be married."

"And I wouldn't want you to, daughter. But the captain, now—"

"The captain!" Carrie tried to sound surprised, though her father's motives had been obvious all afternoon. "Papa, the captain is wedded to the Salvation Army. And why would I want to marry a man like that anyhow, pledged to poverty and service to others? Not that I'm that selfish," she added quickly. "A life of service to others is a fine thing, but . . ."

"But you've had your share of scrimping already. I know that, Carrie. I know I have not provided for you and did not provide for your mother, as I ought to have. And marrying into the Army would not end the scrimping. But you'd always have enough. They would not let you or your children know real want. The captain is a good man, and kind too."

"The captain is a fine man in his way, Papa. I respect him very much, but I do not love him. And even if I did, and even if he wanted to marry me, he couldn't. He said officers can only marry other officers. And I'm not even a member of the Army."

"You could change that, Carrie."

She knew Papa was disappointed that she had not enlisted in the Salvation Army which meant so much to him. "You don't really want me to join the Army just to get a husband, do you, Papa?"

Sam shook his head glumly. "The Army's given me my life, and I'd dearly love to see you a part of it, but only because you've felt the Lord's call."

25

As Carrie snapped the sewing basket closed, Sam spoke again. "But it's only normal for a girl your age to be thinking about marriage."

"Oh, but I do, Papa." She stood, a proud tilt to her head, and turned to the wardrobe in the corner. "Papa, I have to get ready now for the evening service."

Sam took the hint and stepped outside. Carrie drew a muslin curtain around her sleeping cubicle in the kitchen corner and turned in front of the little mirror over the bed. "I do think about getting married," she muttered to herself. "Every girl does, but I'm not stupid. Who's going to want to marry me? I'm not pretty. I'm much too thin, and my nose is too long and doesn't turn up, and my hair's so . . . so brown!"

What she didn't notice, as she buttoned the fresh shirtwaist, was a firm chin, high cheekbones, and deep-set brown eyes that glowed under long golden-brown lashes. *Besides . . .* She tied a jaunty bow at her smooth throat. *Besides, I saw what marriage did to my mother, and I'm not going to let myself be hurt the way she was.*

The big meeting tent was nearly empty that night. The sawdust floor was musty with the dampness. Streams of water dribbled through leaks in the tent roof. Puddles formed, and the heavy mud oozed through the sawdust here and there. Specks of sawdust clung to everyone's wet boots.

Captain Stoneham brought down fire and brimstone upon the few unrepentant who braved the storm to attend. He was beginning to see fruit, take a few captives as the Army put it, among the itinerant workers of the valley. But tonight the captain added another plea, and Carrie knew he was talking to her.

"I think," he urged, his voice more gentle, "that there are some among us who, having received the Lord's blessing and having paid lip service to him, have refused his calling to a holier life. Is there one who, tonight, would answer his call and enlist in his Army to serve him totally?"

The Lord Jesus did die for me, she thought. *He saved me from my sins, has kept me healthy, has provided hope here for a better life for me and my father and brothers. Perhaps the captain is right. Perhaps Papa is right, too, in a way, and the Lord does want me to serve him by joining the Salvation Army.*

The lamplight flickered across John Stoneham's sandy hair, turning it to gold as he bowed his head in prayer. His voice was soft now, pleading. "Lord, look into the hearts of your children, and move them to take their stand for your glory."

I would be safe with him, Carrie thought. *It wouldn't be like it was for my mother. There would always be enough for my children to eat.* It wasn't hard for her to imagine herself ladling out hot soup to the hungry or taking a warm blanket to a poor mother and baby. She knew the joy that helping others could bring. *And I would be serving the Lord too. I ought to want that, after all.*

She was jarred back to reality by the splat of a chaw of tobacco hitting the floor just behind her. She realized the captain was calling again for sinners to come to the penitents' bench in front of the pulpit.

Humph! she reflected. *Serve who? If I were to consider joining the Salvation Army, it would be for just that, to serve the Lord, and not so that I could be considered a potential wife for the captain.*

A harsh grunt came from the direction of the splat. "Hell sounds just fine to me, preacher. Nice and warm and dry. 'Sides, that's where all my pals is goin' to be. I'd be plumb lonesome in that other place."

"Tha's right," a second voice slurred. "Wouldn't know a soul in heaven nohow."

The captain was used to such interruptions. "We're praying for you, brothers. One day you'll know the best Friend man has and be on your way to glory to meet him."

"My friends drink with me. He gonna do that, preacher?"

"Heck, no," another voice spat out behind Carrie. "Man's best friend's a full bottle."

"Father, forgive these lost souls and—"

"Forgive? What's to forgive?"

"Let's give him somethin' to forgive."

As Carrie started to turn toward the troublemakers, something flashed past her ear. She realized, as it crashed against the pulpit, that it was an empty whiskey bottle.

The captain looked up, but before he could speak there was a scuffle. Carrie heard a loud smack and turned to see Matt Hanlon, his face livid with anger, hoisting one of his drinking buddies over his shoulder and carrying him from the tent.

Even Captain Stoneham couldn't recapture his audience after that. Sam, surprisingly, was forgiving as they walked back to their cottage, recalling that he used to treat the Salvation Army preachers much the same way himself.

Carrie was glad enough to get home early and fell asleep thinking of the nice home she'd have someday when she went back to the city and met that nice, steady man with good prospects her mother had told her to wait for.

She was up bright and early the next morning, happy to see the leaden skies turn blue as the white sun rose over the Gabilan Mountains.

Rob and the little boys took off to pick up the team and wagon and round up the other children for school. Sam took shovel and hoe and went to work on the old irrigation ditches left by the mission padres. And Carrie dragged the big galvanized tub half full of rainwater out into the sunshine.

She poured kettles of hot water into the tub from the reservoir on the wood stove, scraped slivers of soap into it, and watched the lather foam. "Thank you, Lord, for rainwater, soft, sweet, and plenty," she whispered, as she dumped the first load of clothes into the tub and began to scrub them on the washboard. She was singing to herself and didn't hear the hoofbeats until the horse slowed in front of the cabin. She tucked damp locks into her cap and untied her sopping apron. As the big redhead dismounted and turned toward her, she noticed flies buzzing around a dirty brown bundle dangling across his saddle.

"Uh, Miss, Miss McLean, is it?"

"I'm Carrie McLean." She was astonished to recognize the brash ranch hand who had introduced himself so rudely that first night, the one who had so forcefully stopped the heckling last night. "Is something wrong?"

she asked. Then she added under her breath, "Something other than your galloping up here, unannounced and uninvited, while I'm doing my washing."

"Oh, no, Miss McLean, nothing's wrong." He twisted his hands, which were obviously unused to idleness. "It's just, well, I wanted to say I'm sorry, about last night, I mean."

"Oh, you are."

"Well, I mean, my buddies kind of got out of hand, cussing and throwing that bottle at the preacher and all."

"The bottle was thrown at the captain, Mr. Hanlon. It is Hanlon, isn't it? Why are you apologizing to me?" Why, she wondered, did this man disturb her so? Somehow, she managed to speak with much more calmness than she felt.

"Well." He twisted his hands again nervously. "Well, I saw the bottle almost hit you, and I knew you were upset. Jack had no right to cause a ruckus like that."

"Salvationists are used to that, Mr. Hanlon," Carrie replied. "We know not everyone wants to hear the gospel."

"That's no cause for interfering with folks that do, though, and I'm right sorry it happened."

He was staring at her, and she could feel every drop of wash water that had splashed on her green plaid gingham dress. It was the one with the long rip in the skirt, too, she remembered. She wondered if he were appraising her mending. "Thank you, Mr. Hanlon, for your apology." He kept looking at her. *Why?* she thought. *Why is he still standing there, staring?*

30

"There's another thing, Miss McLean. I hope you won't take offense," he stammered.

What was the matter with this man? He certainly hadn't been shy that first night at the inn, nor last night at meeting for that matter. Now he was acting like a schoolboy, and Carrie couldn't help but smile at him.

"We, uh, the crew on the ranch I work at, have been hunting down some deer. They come down into the pastures, especially now, when the grass is just starting to come back after the drought, and steal forage from the cattle. So we hunt them. And, well, I hate to see that good meat go to waste, and I thought maybe you folks could use it. I mean, it's not charity or anything like that. Just we got more meat than we can use, and it shouldn't just be left for the coyotes."

"Of course I'm not offended," Carrie assured him. "We appreciate your neighborliness."

"That's it, Miss McLean. Just being neighborly. I could bring you more, if you like, and show you, or maybe your pa, how to dry it so it will keep. It's real good meat."

Carrie recognized the limp brown object, then, for what it was, half a small mule deer, flung skinside up across his cow pony. *Maybe Papa knows how to cut it up,* she thought. After all, Mr. Hanlon did mean to be kind.

She swallowed hard. "I'm sure it is good, Mr. Hanlon. Thank you. We certainly will enjoy it and hope for a chance to repay your kindness."

"And you folks won't be disturbed at your services anymore either. I'll see to that," he promised as he rode off down the muddy lane.

Carrie's face was hot as she returned to her washing and her singing. "Now why did he have to turn up here, of all places, and on wash day?" she muttered. But she had to admit it was good of him to think of them.

Chapter Four

*C*arrie was glad she had her back to the menfolk. She would have surely laughed in Matt Hanlon's face, if she had not been busy doing up the Sunday dinner dishes. Of course, her father had done the courteous thing, inviting Matt to share some of the good venison he kept bringing them, but the man was absurd.

"Moving pictures," he was saying. "Like stereopticon slides, but they move." Will and Tim looked up at him wide-eyed. They sat cross-legged on the rag rug; Rob straddled a kitchen chair backward; and Sam and Matt rocked while Sam encouraged Matt's tall stories.

"People walking around on a big sheet hung up on a wall, big as life," Matt was telling them. "Bigger than life. I saw it myself at the Chicago Exposition."

"I've read about whole towns getting these new electrical lights. Have you seen any of those?" Sam asked.

"Sure have. They're lots brighter than gas lights even, and safer too."

Sounds wonderful, Carrie thought. *I wish I believed him, but I'm sure I'll be trimming kerosene lamps as long as I live.*

"I saw a horseless carriage once, when we lived in San Francisco," Rob said.

"I rode in one once," Matt told him. "That was in Chicago too."

"I'm not sure those will catch on, Matt. Awfully noisy, smelly gadgets."

"That's so, Sam, but I think that can be fixed. They can be made to run a lot faster than horses and pull heavier loads. Think, Sam, what it would mean if we could haul our harvests to San Francisco in one day, instead of three. We could grow truck crops and get them to market before they spoil. And cheap too. No more having to pay the railroads whatever they asked to ship our crops. We could just load our produce on a gas-powered wagon right in the field and take it directly to our customers."

That sounded familiar, Carrie thought. *Papa was going to buy a farm near Oakland once and haul the produce by ferry. Now Matt was fueling those same tired dreams.* Carrie bit her lip to keep from interrupting.

"If we had one of those steam tractors we could plow up this clay better."

"Sure could, Sam. I worked on a farm in Kansas that had one. We could plow forty acres a day. Used it with the mower too. I remember one day we felt a storm coming on, and we hooked that rig up and got in the hay in the nick of time. Would have lost half the crop if we'd had to use a team."

"You've sure been everywhere, haven't you, Matt?" Rob's chin dropped. "I've never seen any place but San Francisco and here."

"Well, Rob, it's all still there waiting for you. But right here's the best place I've found so far."

"Where are you actually from, Matt?" Sam inquired. "Back east somewhere, I suspect?"

"Born in Pittsburgh, Sam. I've been working my way west the past ten years or so."

"Ten years! You must have started out when you were in knickers."

"Just about. I guess I was fourteen, maybe fifteen."

"How come your pa let you quit school? Mine says I got to go all the way through high school." Will made it sound like forever. Maybe to a ten year old it was.

"Your pa's right, Willy. But I didn't have a pa, you see. I never knew my ma or pa. I grew up in an orphans' home. So when I figured I was big enough to work, I just left one day and started walking west."

"I never had a ma either, Mr. Hanlon," Tim said wistfully. "But Carrie took care of me."

"You're a lucky boy there, Tim. I didn't have a pretty sister, either."

Pretty, Carrie thought. *He hasn't been around that much, if he thinks I'm pretty.* Still, it was nice to hear it. Again, Carrie was glad the men were behind her as she felt her cheeks flush.

"How come you settled down here, Matt?" Sam asked. "I'd have thought an ambitious young fellow like you would have picked a city."

"I don't know as how I've settled exactly. But I think I do want a farm. I worked in Chicago quite a while. There were lots of odd jobs during the Exposition. But then I got tired of it and went on to Kansas. That's where I found out I liked getting my hands into the soil. Liked watching the seeds sprout and the wheat grow and turn into gold. It feels good, smells good."

"Yup." Sam thumped the table with a soil-stained fist. "That's for me too."

"Did you ever farm before, Sam?"

"Never did. I grew up in the gold fields, with my dad. He had a farm, not far from Chicago, as a matter of fact. But he sold it to follow the forty-niners. Like most of them he always just missed the big strike, and he regretted 'til the day he died selling that farm. I guess that's why I always wanted one."

"Not me," Rob exploded. "I had enough of this place the first week."

"That's just because we're having some rough times, son. When we get some crops growing and a little cash coming in, you'll get to like it."

That was more of Sam's dreaming, Carrie knew. And it was obvious to her that Rob was growing more discontented every day.

"You are seeing the Salinas Valley at its worst, Rob. When I first rode in, a couple of years ago, it was a fine place. The rain had been good; the river was running; and every young fellow willing to work had silver in his pockets."

"I've tried to find work, Matt. But nobody's hiring," Rob grumbled.

"Not now, but it will be like that again next spring," Matt promised. "All we need is a good season of rain. I've been here in the good times, Rob, and they'll come back."

Carrie dried the last pot and turned around. "And what makes you so sure, Mr. Hanlon, that this winter will be a good one?"

"Miss Carrie." Matt smiled that self-confident smile of his. "I'm not a religious person like you folks, but I figure the good Lord knows we need it."

"Amen to that. He brought us here, and he's going to look after us. Now, Timmy, your sister's been working hard all day. You carry out that dishwater for her."

"It's all right, Pa. I want to put it on the vegetable patch. It's been more than a month since those good fall rains you're so pleased about," she reminded them. "And my garden's drying up again."

Rob was very quiet the rest of the day. On Monday he took the children to school in the Salvation Army's wagon and left again to bring them home as dusk fell. But when Will and Tim came in, Rob was not with them. "Did Rob drop you off before he took the team back to the barn?"

"Uh, no, Carrie." Will twisted his book strap.

Tim studied the cracks in the plank floor. "Carrie, Rob didn't bring us home."

"What do you mean, Timmy? Where is Rob?"

"What about Rob?" Sam asked as he stomped in, shaking the heavy clay from his boots. "Something wrong with the team or the wagon?"

"No, Pa. Nothing like that," Will assured him. "Rob said to tell you not to worry."

"Not worry about what, Will?"

"Not to worry about him, Pa. He told me to drive the wagon back and put the team up and to tell you not to worry."

"You drove the wagon back, Will?" Carrie couldn't believe Rob would be so irresponsible as to turn over a valuable team and wagon, not to mention all the schoolchildren, to a ten-year-old boy. By doing so he would probably lose his job, and they needed his little bit of pay to make ends meet. "Rob wouldn't let you do that."

Timmy nodded. "He said Will could drive us. He said to tell you he was going up to Salinas City."

Will interrupted. "He told me to tell them, not you. You're too little to get it right."

"Quit bickering and tell me what your brother said," Sam demanded.

"Yes, Pa. Rob said to tell you he was going up to Salinas City to find work, and you weren't to worry, and he'd let you know as soon as he found something."

"Is that all?" Carrie tried to read more on their confused faces. "Just that he was going to Salinas to look for work and would let us know?" She thought of all the families whose sons had left, promising to write, and how few had ever been heard from again. She knew from his troubled frown that her father was thinking of the same thing.

"And just how did he plan to get to Salinas City?" Sam asked.

Will's lips quivered. "He said something about the trains, Pa."

"Where'd he get the money for the train?"

"He didn't need any, Papa. He said lots of guys just hopped onto a passing freight train and—"

"Stealing a ride! A son of mine riding the rails!"

"Aw, Pa. Lots of fellows do it." Will shrugged. "Mr. Hanlon said he's done it lots of times."

"Mr. Hanlon said, did he?" Carrie snapped. "You see what happens, Pa, when you invite a man like that into your home, a man with no breeding, no background, no manners. Now he's talked Rob into running off Lord knows where and—"

"Carrie, it's probably not that bad. I expect the lad will find honest work up there and be riding back one day in a paid seat to tell us about it, or he'll hitch a ride back the same way he went and be none the worse for the experience."

Sam was right, this time. A week later Rob rode up to the cabin just before supper. The nag he was using looked pretty worn-out, and he explained that she was borrowed. "This guy I met said I could use her to come home to say good-bye."

"Good-bye? But, Rob, you just got home. You're not leaving again right away," exclaimed Sam.

"Yes, I am, Pa. I have to be in San Francisco in three days. Pa, Carrie, I'm off to war."

"To war? To Cuba?"

"Wherever. Anyhow, I've joined the army."

"Sit down, son, and let's talk this over." Sam and Rob sat across the kitchen table from each other as Carrie ladled out the steaming venison stew.

Sam continued, "You know, joining the army's a pretty serious step."

"I know, Pa. But I've just got to get out of here. I just can't see myself as a farmer, and I've looked and looked for a job. Nobody's hiring up in Salinas City either, because of the drought and the hard times. And the army's a good deal. I'll get to see some country, maybe Cuba or the Philippines if Spain isn't licked before I get out of camp. And it pays twelve dollars a month and my keep."

"And you'll get to sleep in a tent and shoot big guns."

"Sure will, Tim."

"Will you see Teddy Roosevelt?" Will wondered.

Rob laughed at his little brothers' eager questions. "I don't expect I'll see the colonel, Will. He's too busy for raw recruits like me. But who knows?"

"Robbie, my boy, have you really thought about this?" Sam pressed. "It might sound exciting, but I have a feeling it's a lot of hard work and rough company."

"I'm not afraid of either one, Pa."

"Why didn't you talk this over with us before you went off and enlisted?" Carrie asked.

"I hadn't really decided before I went to Salinas, Carrie. Sure, I'd thought about it—charging up a hill on a fast horse and watching those Spaniards run."

"Sometimes they shoot back," she retorted. "Robbie, people get killed in battles."

"I know that. I know it's not really all excitement," Rob conceded. "But there I was in Salinas, knocking on doors and getting told there wasn't any work. And here was a steady, respectable job, a good-looking uniform, and a train ticket out."

"And you're sure it's what you want to do?" Sam persisted.

"Yes, Pa, I'm sure. Besides, it's all settled. I report to Fort Mason on Friday."

It had been hard seeing Rob ride off, especially just before the holidays. Now it was Thanksgiving, and the Fort Romie settlers had invited their Soledad neighbors to a celebration of the season. *Rob should be out there pitching,* Carrie thought, as she cheered on the Salvation Army baseball team.

"Of course, we've no harvests yet," a neighbor said to Anna Arnesen, "but we've lots of hope, I guess."

"Maybe that's more important than the harvest itself," Anna answered. "Sometimes I think it's hope that keeps us all going."

"You sound like Papa, Anna." Carrie had heard Anna's words and joined the conversation.

"Your papa's a good man, Carrie. He works hard, and he needs his hopes to keep him going."

"He does work hard, Anna. I know he does, but he has so little to show for it."

"He has three strong sons and a lovely daughter. Why have you so many doubts, Carrie?"

"Probably because Pa has so few. Someone has to be realistic." She noticed Sam had come up to bat. "Come on, Pa. A good hit and we beat them."

Anna nodded. "Now that's what I call being realistic. You're behind five to seven with two outs in the last inning."

"But the bases are loaded," Carrie reminded her.

The bat connected with a loud crack, and it was Harold Arnesen, Anna's husband, who missed the catch that let the Fort Romie team win. "See." Carrie chuckled. "You were right. There's always hope." Anna's lusty laugh joined Carrie's.

"Who were you rooting for anyhow?" Mr. Arnesen asked his wife as he joined them at the long picnic table. "Carrie's father just drove in the winning run for the other side, and my own wife is grinning from ear to ear."

"You proved a point for me, Harold. I was just telling Carrie that hope was what kept us alive."

"Hope and a little sun in my eyes. Hey, McLean, come here and join these beautiful ladies."

"Soon as I find the youngsters, Harold."

Will, Tim, and Eric Arnesen, like all small boys, could smell fried rabbit from any place in the county. They were at the table before Sam could spot his sons' carrot tops or tow-headed Eric. But Sam did spot another redhead. And when he came back to the table he brought Matt Hanlon with him.

"Mmmm. Fried rabbit and corn bread. Thanks for inviting me, Sam."

"Just a preview of years to come, Matt. Once we get this place going, our harvest festivals will be famous. Harold's been telling me how these Danes grow barley with no more water than the fog brings."

42

"They grow wheat that way up in the Dakotas. I met a fellow in Kansas who told me about it. Ten inches of rain a year's all it takes, if you know how."

"Last year we got less than eight," Carrie interrupted.

"But, Miss Carrie, that was an unusually bad year. Most years we get twelve or fifteen," Mr. Arnesen explained patiently. "That's plenty."

Carrie felt properly reproved for interrupting a conversation about something she wasn't supposed to know anything about. Besides, Matt Hanlon was bragging again about the wonders he'd seen in his travels, so Carrie went back to tending her little brothers' table manners and pretending not to listen.

"Dry farming's okay for grains, if there's no prolonged drought," he was saying. "But the answer to this valley's problem is irrigation."

"It's been tried, Matt. We've dug wells, and the Mexicans before us dug wells, but we're lucky to get drinking water for ourselves and a milk cow, let alone enough for a herd of cattle or to irrigate crops."

"Those were shallow wells, Harold, dug by hand. I'm talking about deep wells," Matt explained. "They're drilled with steam engines."

"And the water's pumped by windmills. A rancher down King City way has one." Mr. Arnesen shook his head. "But it costs a lot of money, and how do we know there's water there at all?"

"There's water," Sam insisted. "I knew there was water first time I saw all the willow trees. They can't live without plenty of water."

That's Papa, Carrie thought, *always trying to prove his point by quoting some irrelevant fact.*

But Matt Hanlon was just as bad. "Right you are, Sam. Where there are willows, there's water. In fact, my boss is bringing in a steam drill and crew in the spring to put in some wells on his ranch."

Chapter Five

Will you be finished with your reading soon, Papa?" Carrie hinted, as she set her sewing basket on the table.

Sam laid his Bible aside. "Did you want to talk, Carrie?"

"I'd like to move the lamp closer, please. I still have the buttonholes to finish on the boys' new shirts, and with all the baking to do tomorrow and the chicken to clean and stuff, I want to get the shirts finished tonight."

"Sure, any time. The reading will wait, but the shirts must be finished tonight. After all, tomorrow is Christmas Eve." He fingered the soft gray serge, and Carrie wished, with all her heart, that there had been enough for a shirt for her father too. "I hate to see you give up your beautiful skirt, Carrie."

"I don't need things like that here. It was an extravagance even when I was working at the Emporium, but here it was just packed away to rot. It's much better to use the fabric for something the boys really need."

"Well, I sure hope Will and Timmy appreciate it—both the fabric and the hard work." He sighed as he put the Bible back into its box. "I wish I had something for them."

"We've an orange each and nuts for their stockings. And I'll make fudge tomorrow."

"Yes, but they're just little boys. Some plaything, something just for fun—a ball and bat, a storybook."

"They understand. They know there is no money for store-bought gifts. We're lucky, Papa. We've got a fat rooster outside to kill for a good Christmas dinner. We have got flour, lard, and sugar enough for bread and cookies, and there'll be dried apple pie for dessert."

"Thanks to the Arnesens. I still don't feel quite right about taking that chicken. What have we done to deserve such neighbors?"

"They are good neighbors. And Anna insisted Rob had earned the chicken helping Harold re-roof their barn last summer."

"I wonder what kind of Christmas Rob will have in New Jersey in that army camp," Sam said.

"Probably turkey and sweet potatoes and even mince-meat pie," Carrie assured him. "There will be lots of other new recruits there too. I imagine they'll have a church service and sing carols tomorrow night just like we will."

"He'll be lonesome, all the same."

"At least he won't have to think about getting shot, now that Spain has sued for peace. Thank God for that."

"Amen, Carrie."

She knotted the thread and began sewing the tiny buttons on the shirts. Sam rocked quietly for a few minutes and then cleared his throat. "Ah, Carrie, I was thinking about Rob being alone for Christmas. There's lots of other young men who don't have families to spend Christmas with either. Some of the young farmhands around here, for instance."

"For instance?" She knew what he was getting at, of course.

"Well, young Hanlon, for instance. I like that fellow. He's going to go places."

"Oh, you think so?" As she bit off the thread she muttered under her breath. "Just where do you think he's going? Straight to the dickens if you want my opinion."

"You don't like Matt Hanlon much, do you?"

"Should I?" She spoke more loudly than usual to drown out the unwelcome thumping of her heart. "He's rude, a braggart, full of big talk with nothing behind it."

"He's been mannerly enough when he's been here, unless there's something you've not told me, Carrie."

He gave her a worried look, and in honesty she had to reassure him. "Oh, no, Papa. He's never done anything he shouldn't have." Except, maybe, she added to herself, that first night at the inn. Even then he'd barely touched her arm. The real trouble with Matt, she admitted to herself, was that he was too nice to her.

Sam looked relieved. "Then why does he annoy you?"

"He talks on so, about what he's seen and done," she rationalized. "That's what sent Rob off, you know."

"Could be," Sam admitted. "But, you see, I'm not so sure Rob didn't do the right thing. The army won't hurt the boy, Carrie. Even if Matt did, in some way, suggest it, it may be the best thing that could have happened."

47

"But what about the farm? I thought you wanted your sons to build a farm with you that you could pass on to them."

"There's lots of time for that. Rob will be back. And, if not, Rob has a right to his own dreams, Carrie."

"Dreams, always dreams. Papa, you live on yours, and Matt Hanlon lives on his. That's the way you are, I guess, but the dreams aren't real. I can't see them or taste them or touch them, like you seem to be able to."

Carrie realized her father's eyes were watering as he replied. "Nor could your mother. I know she couldn't. I tried to make them real for her, to make them come true. But something always went wrong. I saved up and bought a team, and one of the horses went lame. I got a good job, and then I broke my leg and couldn't work. We were getting back on our feet. We really were, and then she took sick after Timmy came, and the doctor bills took all I could earn. I tried, Carrie."

"I know you tried, Papa. She loved you for trying, and I love you for trying. I didn't mean to criticize."

"But you don't like Matt because he's like me."

He was right. Carrie saw, in Matt Hanlon, the Sam McLean her mother had talked about, the Sam McLean who had courted Liz and won her with his dreams.

Carrie tilted her head and lifted a firm chin as she spoke. "All right. Matt Hanlon is your friend. He's welcome in your house. If you invite him for Christmas dinner, I'll be civil."

"I know you will, Carrie. Now, it's my bedtime."

"Good night, Papa." As she turned down the quilt on her bed in the kitchen corner, Carrie muttered her own

48

resolve. "He's welcome in your house, but he needn't bother complimenting me, nor think he can come courting." She remembered again her mother's words: "Never marry a man who dreams."

The next evening the big tent was brightly lighted for the Christmas Eve meeting. Someone had hauled a great pine tree around the mountain from Monterey and festooned it with strings of popcorn and bright red fruits from the native manzanita bushes. Popcorn balls, frosted ginger cookies, and candied apples hung from the branches. A couple of dozen wrapped packages lay arranged under the boughs.

"Some people in the city sent gifts for the children," Sister Addie whispered, noticing Carrie's puzzled look.

Carrie bristled at the idea of her brothers taking such charity, but Sam only smiled and said, "Wasn't it nice of them to think of our youngsters that way?"

As they waited for Captain Stoneham to open the service, Carrie looked around. The tent was nearly full, for many of their neighbors had joined the celebration of the Lord's birth. Carrie waved to the Arnesens and Svensens across the aisle.

Eric whispered something to his mother and then came over to the McLeans. "Can Will and Tim go up with me to look at the Christmas tree, please?" he asked.

"Go ahead," Sam said, "but come right back here and sit down quietly the minute the music starts."

Carrie was happy to see so many Soledad people at the service but saddened at how few of the Fort Romie colonists remained. Three families had left that first day.

Two more had gone before the cabins were finished. Now, since Thanksgiving, Tom Jeffries had heard of work in Oakland and taken his family there, and Susanna Meadows's father had sent train fare for them to join him on his farm in Iowa. Less than two-thirds of them were left, after only three months.

Carrie saw Matt slip into a seat in the back row. *At least he's alone*, she thought. It was, after all, his rowdy friends who had disrupted the meetings.

Carrie joined in the Christmas singing eagerly. The music was beautiful; the children were as restless and exited as, well, as children on Christmas Eve; her heart was warmed, as every heart must be, remembering the Holy Babe who gave himself to the world that first Christmas.

As always, when the captain finished his preaching, he invited the sinners present to accept God's gift of forgiveness. Few seekers had come to the penitents' bench since the founding of the Fort Romie Corps, but the Army never stopped inviting them.

Carrie heard the scratch of a chair and the scuffle of heavy boots behind her and realized a man was coming forward. As he passed their row Carrie heard her papa's "Praise the Lord" and looked up to see Matt's red head bowed humbly as he strode to the front of the tent.

Papa's was not the only voice of praise for Matt's conversion, for his open-handed good nature had made him popular with the colony already.

Of course Carrie was pleased too. *Shouldn't I rejoice, as the angels in heaven are said to, when a lost soul is saved?*

And that, she insisted to herself, *is my only concern in the matter.*

She had reconciled herself to hearing, over Christmas dinner, all the details of the soul-searching and miraculous visions that had preceded Matt Hanlon's conversion. She was sure that, at the very least, he would already be dreaming of the day he would open darkest Africa or heathen China to the work of the Salvation Army. Carrie was surprised by his simple testimony.

"I'm not sure just why I did it, Sam. I was sitting there thinking about the nuns in the orphanage lighting their candles and about how everything I had I'd gotten by the sweat of my brow. Suddenly I knew I was wrong. I hadn't earned any good thing. I couldn't. I could try, and I guess I'll always try, but without God's help it's all pipe dreams."

"Matt, I'm just brimming over with joy for you. I couldn't be happier if you were my own son. Now that you've found the Lord while you're young, you have a whole lifetime to live with him."

"Your example was part of it, Sam. I'd never seen your kind of faith before. I was baptized and confirmed. Even went to Mass once a year, more or less, after I ran away from the home. I was scared of God, so I tried to obey the rules. But I never heard of knowing Jesus, as a friend, until I met you people."

"I was already an old man when I learned that," Sam sighed. "I was a dreamer, like you, Matt. I still am, and I hope you'll keep hold of your dreams too. But I wasted most of my life trying to make them come true on my own. You have got the chance to be God's partner."

"You have to say your prayers every night when you're a Christian, Mr. Hanlon. Then he gives you what you ask for," Tim offered.

"Sometimes he does, Tim, when you ask for the right things," Carrie gently corrected.

"He gave me my own baseball bat, Carrie. That's what I wanted, and I asked him for one."

"Some nice people in the city sent that because . . ." She hesitated, not wanting to say, "because their little boy didn't want it anymore," but she couldn't spoil Timmy's Christmas. Instead she continued firmly, "Because Jesus told them how to make a little boy very happy on Christmas."

"It's no less an answer to prayer because it came through someone's generosity, Carrie," Sam put in. "It's his doing, just as the Salvation Army making this land available to us is his doing."

Carrie wanted to ask why God didn't include a reliable water supply, but, after all, it was Christmas.

"Yes, sir," Sam continued. "I knew as soon as I heard about the plans for Fort Romie that it was the good Lord's answer to my prayers. I'd been trying to save for a farm all my life. Then I got saved, started walking his way, turned the dream over to him, and here we are."

"I'm used to getting things on my own," Matt admitted. "That's pride, and it's going to be hard to swallow mine and rely on him, but I know it's right, and I'm going to do my best."

"Of course we owe God all we have," Carrie conceded, "but don't you think the old saying is pretty much true, that the Lord helps those who help themselves?"

"No doubt he does, Miss Carrie. He must expect us to use the abilities he gave us and not just sit back and wait for manna to fall out of heaven. If you want a farm to produce, you've got to plow and sow, weed and pick. But it's still God who makes the crops grow."

"Or not grow, Mr. Hanlon." Her fears forced the harsh words out. "Sometimes, despite all the work and all the prayers, the rains don't come and the crops don't grow."

"Hey, I don't have all the answers, Miss Carrie. I'm new at this faith thing." He smiled gently, and his cool blue eyes twinkled.

"I'm sorry. I shouldn't have said that. I don't want to discourage you. It's just that I see so many people, good Christian people, who work and pray as hard as they can and are still poor."

"Of course, poor is relative. I mean, you're poor, but you just put a feast on the table for Christmas, so you're not starving, like a lot of folks are. I never heard that God promised we'd be rich, not on earth anyhow. He just said we'd have enough."

"Matt's right," Sam agreed. "The Lord promised enough, and we have that, Carrie. We have a good roof over our heads and food on the table."

She had to admit her father was right for the moment, but Carrie couldn't get rid of her nagging doubts. "Then let's pray fervently for some more rain to keep it that way."

"Let's go one better, Miss Carrie. Let's pray for better than rain. Let's pray for wells, so we'll have water month after month, year after year. I believe that's what God really wants to give us, if we just have the faith to ask for it and work for it."

Chapter Six

The colonists' Christmas prayers for renewed rain were bountifully answered in January. It rained steadily for nearly a week, soaking into the caked adobe and turning it to black muck. But a week of fair weather followed, and every man and horse in the valley turned out to work the moist soil and replant the withered crops.

Sam had helped Harold Arnesen replant the sugar beets he planned to sell at the new sugar mill up in Salinas, and in return Mr. Arnesen lent his team so Sam could replant his wheat field. Matt offered his Saturday afternoon off to help with the planting. No doubt he and Sam were telling each other how many bushels they would harvest, come summer, Carrie guessed, as she mashed potatoes for supper.

"Hurry up, Matt. I smell beans baking," Sam shouted, as he scraped his boots outside the door. He sniffed deeply as he came into the kitchen. "Isn't it enough that the man gives up his half-day off to help me, without his bringing his own supper?"

"What supper?" Matt tried to look innocent as he hung his jacket over a chair back. "I just brought along a hunk of side pork. I delivered a load of beef to the butcher a couple of days ago, and he was practically giving the side meat away."

"We do appreciate it, Mr. Hanlon, but, as Papa says, you are too generous with both your time and money."

"Pure selfishness, Miss Carrie. I've never smelled baked beans like yours."

"Why, thank you, Mr. Hanlon." His compliments made her as uncomfortable as his generosity. "The beans will be done in fifteen minutes or so." She quickly changed the subject. "Papa, where are Tim and Will?"

"Taking the team home."

"Now? They'll be starved by the time they walk all that way back."

"They won't be long. Matt let them take his horse to ride home."

"Sell off that wheat come summer, and you can buy a horse yourself, Sam," Matt suggested.

"Maybe. Sort of thinking of a milk cow, though. And there'll be the hundred dollars due on the land."

"You folks sure got a good deal on the place. I wish I could get myself a farm for ten dollars an acre a year. Even on my wages I could save up a hundred for a down payment."

"How about one of the empty plots here?" Sam suggested. "Several families have pulled out."

"But the Salvation Army's still trying to resettle the poor from the city. You know, 'the manless land for the landless man.' I guess they aren't worried about poor country people as much as poor city people."

Hearing the sound of the boys' arrival, Matt turned his attention to the door. "Did you rub Tramp down good, boys?" Matt asked, as Will and Tim let the door slam behind them.

"Yes, Mr. Hanlon. And gave him the bag of oats like you said."

As Carrie dished out the steaming beans and side pork, Sam returned to the subject of a farm for Matt. "Have you asked the captain about buying one of those places, Matt?"

"As a matter of fact, I did mention it one Sunday on the way into Soledad for the street preaching. But, as he pointed out, that land doesn't actually belong to the Army now. Those folks that put down their hundred dollars don't lose their farms until they miss their payment next harvest time. And by then I expect there'll be more city folks eager to try farming."

"Why would you want to buy a farm, Mr. Hanlon?" Tim asked. "Isn't it more fun being a cowboy?"

"Being a cowboy's all right for boys." Matt smiled at Tim's question. "But there comes a time a man wants to settle down. Yes, I'd like to have a farm of my own."

"Here, in this valley, Mr. Hanlon? Why, with all the places you've seen, do you want a farm in a place that alternates between burning drought and deluge?" Carrie wondered aloud.

"Now, Miss Carrie, you've only been here a few months. It isn't always like this. And it's going to get better."

"Anna told me there's been drought two years of the past three. The Arnesens have been dry-farming their land on shares for ten years and still haven't saved enough to buy it."

"They'll make money off the beets they're putting in. Big money," Matt assured her.

"If the rains keep up, but not too much, of course."

"I can't deny farming's risky business, Miss Carrie, but once we get those deep wells dug we won't have to worry about drought."

"Matt's right, Carrie," Sam insisted. "I just know the good Lord gave me this piece of ground, and he's not going to let us starve on it, nor lose it."

"I hope and pray you are right, Papa, but I've seen a lot of good Christian people go hungry." Carrie had seen her father's hopes dashed so many times before that she couldn't hide her fears. "Just because you two have all these dreams doesn't mean God is going to make them come true."

"Why do you always expect the worst, Miss Carrie?" She felt the hairs stand up on the back of her neck as they always did when those eyes looked at her and through her. "Mark my words, Miss Carrie. That water's waiting down there under the willow trees. It's just waiting for us to bring it up. When we do the whole valley's going to bloom like the land of Canaan. And when it does, I know the Lord intends me to have a piece of it."

Carrie wanted to believe him. *If only he had that farm; if only he could offer* . . . Carrie abruptly excused herself and put the teakettle on to heat dishwater. *Don't be silly,* she told herself. *He hasn't offered you anything. And he hasn't got anything to offer you anyhow.*

The next Sunday evening after meeting, Captain Stoneham asked if he could see Carrie home. It had been several weeks since he had singled her out in any way, so Carrie was surprised, and a little disturbed, by the request. She looked at her father, hoping for an excuse, but he just waved and said he'd see her later.

The little congregation dispersed; Lieutenant Margaret and Sister Addie offered to straighten up the meeting tent; and Carrie and Captain Stoneham started up the damp dirt lane.

"Miss Carrie," he began, "I have noticed over these months your fine character. You are a very capable young woman, spirited but faithful."

"Why thank you, Captain," she murmured, but he appeared not to have heard. She suspected he was repeating a practiced speech.

"You are an attractive young woman and, I have observed, an accomplished housekeeper as well. In short, Miss Carrie, I have found in my life no other young woman so suitable."

Suitable, she thought. It was an interesting choice of words—certainly not the one Matt would have used.

"Except for one detail, of course," Captain Stoneham continued. "Miss Carrie, I had not planned to speak to you so soon, hoping you would feel called to serve the Lord before I did so. But I have received notice of my departure. I shall be leaving here in only two weeks, and so I have . . ."

Carrie tried not to sound relieved as she interrupted. "Oh, what a shame, Captain. We shall miss you."

"Yes, yes. Lieutenant Margaret will be leaving after her wedding, as you know, and I expect a married couple will be sent here to replace me."

He seemed to be in a hurry to get back to his prepared speech. "I have asked your father's permission to declare my affection. As you know, an officer in the Salvation Army may marry only with the Army's approval and may only marry another officer. However, if you would be willing to accept my offer of marriage, I should be quite willing to wait for you to meet the necessary conditions."

How very noble of him, Carrie thought. She was glad it was too dark for him to see her amusement. "Captain Stoneham, I am humbled that you would consider me suitable to be your wife. It is a great compliment." She knew that it was. "But I have given no thought to such a thing. Nor do I feel I have been called by the Lord even to enlist in the Salvation Army, much less to become an officer."

"I would hope you might consider my proposal such a call, Miss Carrie. I can assure you that he, in his love, will never fail you. And I, too, love you and pledge to seek your happiness."

He meant it, she knew, and she was touched by his carefully rehearsed declaration. Besides, as her father had said to her last fall, the captain was a kind and reliable gentleman, and the Army would never let them starve.

It wasn't anything like the proposals she had whispered about with her girlfriends back in the city. But she remembered the "proper" response they had rehearsed even then, and it seemed appropriate now. "Captain Stoneham, you do me a great honor, but I just don't know what to say. I really must have a little time to think about this."

Lieutenant Margaret's fiancé came down from Oakland, and they were married in the big tent the following Wednesday evening. Carrie had promised herself that she would give the captain his answer that night.

She had also promised herself that she would seriously consider his proposal, and she was still considering it as she watched the simple marriage ceremony. *After all, I really don't have that many options,* she reasoned. *I can't keep house for Papa all my life. Even now the boys are big enough that I'm not that desperately needed. I could go back to San Francisco and support myself, but I have no money for school. Why, that's as much an idle dream as Papa's, or*—she caught her breath sharply—*Matt's.*

I could probably marry Matt Hanlon, she realized with a prickle of excitement. *Oh, no. I'm not going to let myself be taken in by his big talk. Maybe if he did have a farm of his own, but he's worse than Papa with his wild ideas and empty pockets.*

I could enlist, she calculated, *and, after a year or so as a faithful servant of the Lord and Commissioner Booth-Tucker, be permitted to marry Captain Stoneham. As a dutiful soldier and wife I would certainly be rewarded in heaven. That was something to be considered. And it would not be such a bad life.*

Captain Stoneham stood facing Margaret and her soon-to-be husband. *I wouldn't call the captain handsome,* Carrie pondered. But he did look almost noble in his dark blue uniform trimmed with red and gold. He was clean-shaven, with his sandy brown hair closely cropped. His slender hands gestured gracefully as he preached the wedding sermon. She could almost see herself standing to one side of the lectern in her dark poke bonnet, playing her cornet as he led congregational singing. She could do worse.

The ceremony had ended. Margaret stood with her husband accepting the congratulations of their friends. But as she nodded and smiled thanks, she kept looking up into his face. And as she did, Carrie saw the glow on Margaret's face, the tears of joy in her eyes. She saw that look of love, and she felt a desperate need to know that joy for herself someday. And she knew she could never look at Captain John Stoneham with the utter rapture she saw in Margaret.

The captain stood beside her, and gently touched her arm. "Miss Carrie," he asked softly, "have you an answer for me yet?"

He probably thinks I have been so moved by the occasion that I will see myself as a bride, she reflected. *I don't want to hurt him.*

"Captain, I have given your proposal careful consideration." Maybe it was a stock answer, but she really had considered it, she assured herself. "I appreciate your offer. I have a great deal of respect for you and for the Salvation

Army as well. But for that reason I feel it would be very wrong for me to mock the Army by joining it in order to marry you."

"Your honesty, Miss Carrie, is one of your most endearing qualities. You are right, of course. Such a thing would be a mockery. Yet I would be a false servant were I to leave my work for any woman, even you."

"Oh, Captain Stoneham!" Her fervor was real, though not for the reasons he would guess. "John, I would never let you consider such a thing."

Chapter Seven

The day after Captain Stoneham left, the heavens opened. It seemed as if God, in some fit of perverse humor, chose to mock their earlier prayers. For four days the rain came down in windblown sheets like cold, stiff, gray sails.

At Matt's suggestion, Sam had replanted his fields so that the plants grew in raised rows and the rushing water coursed between them. Some of the other colonists had not heeded the advice. Now they watched as the tiny seedlings once again washed away in the flood.

The cabins were rough, but they were stoutly built to ward off the howling storm. The cistern and wash tubs were all filled with the precious soft water, and they could expect the shallow wells to be full through the next summer if the rest of the rainy season were anywhere near normal.

"And we thank thee, Lord, for the rains you have sent to us this week," Sam said. "Amen. Please pass the bread, Will."

"Eric says the river's rising, Pa," Will said as he handed the loaf to his father.

"I'll bet it is, son. It should run deep well into the summer if this keeps up."

"Eric said his pa told him to warn us about flooding."

"Oh, Will, we're miles from the river and on high ground," Carrie reassured her brother.

"He says the river's tricky when it gets high, Carrie. But I guess he didn't mean our place was in any danger," Will conceded.

The next day, Saturday, dawned sunny, though there were still towering clouds to the south. The wind had almost stopped. When Will and Tim asked to go and check their scattered rabbit traps, Carrie shooed them off, glad to have them out from underfoot so she could scrub the floors in peace.

They and Sam had tracked in half of the outside mud, it seemed, and Carrie rolled up her sleeves and plunged into her housecleaning. She was startled when the door slammed and she heard her father's voice.

"What's for lunch, Carrie?"

"It can't be noon already, Papa."

"Sure is. Clouding up for another shower too."

Carrie looked out the front window to see a pale sun peeking through an ominous thunderhead. "I'll put on the coffeepot and slice some bread and cheese, Papa. I'm surprised the boys aren't home."

"They said something this morning about checking their traps with Eric and having lunch at the Arnesens," Sam explained.

"They asked to check the traps, but they didn't say anything to me about the Arnesens."

"They mentioned it to me on their way past the tool shed," Sam told her. "I hope they come on home after lunch, though, before that new storm hits."

By mid-afternoon it was nearly dark, and the rain was falling hard again. Carrie stared out the window as she kneaded her bread dough. "Those kids know better than to stay out in this," she mused.

Sam stuck his head out the door for the hundredth time. "I thought I heard a wagon coming. Maybe Harold's driving them home."

"I didn't hear anything but the wind and the rain." Carrie set the half-full bread pans on the warming shelf to rise and listened again. "Yes, there is someone coming."

"Those boys are going to get a whipping this time." Sam strode toward the door, but they heard Harold Arnesen's shout before he reached it. "Eric, you here?"

Mr. Arnesen drained his broad-brimmed hat and shook his macintosh before he came in. "You mean those youngsters aren't here either?" he questioned.

"They should have come home right away when they saw there was another storm coming," Carrie said.

"Now, don't panic, Carrie." Mr. Arnesen's voice was less than convincing as he continued. "They're smart kids. They probably holed up somewhere safe when the rain started and will come dashing in as soon as it lets up."

Sam reached for his heavy sweater. "It's already dark, Harold. They can't be left out there all night."

Mr. Arnesen nodded. "Going to be next to impossible to find them in the dark, Sam."

"I suppose so, but we've got to try. Carrie, get a couple of lanterns filled for me."

"Be careful, Papa," she begged, as the two worried fathers started out into the darkness.

"We'll find them and be back in no time." Sam paused. "Pray that we do, daughter."

As they started toward Mr. Arnesen's horse and the one he had led for Eric, Carrie heard Sam say, "Let's stop by for Matt Hanlon, Harold. He helped the boys locate the trap line, so he'll know better than us where to start looking."

Sam didn't have to remind his daughter to pray. Somehow it had never seemed right to her to ask God for groceries or rent money. But surely God cared about the safety of her little brothers. He wouldn't let them be hurt out there in the storm. Besides, Matt could find them. Matt could also get other men to help, men with horses from the ranch. And Matt knew where the traps were.

Carrie tried to keep busy. She started peas soaking for some thick, hot soup. She baked the bread and kept the coffeepot hot on the stove. She tried to do the mending but spent more time pacing the floor than plying her needle. She opened the big Bible to read, rested her head on its pages to pray, and dozed intermittently.

She roused to the tramping of feet and babble of voices. Sam came in with Matt right behind him, each carrying an exhausted boy in his arms.

"Pa, are they all right?"

"The boys are fine, Carrie," Sam replied, "except that they're soaking wet and worn-out."

"I have dry nightshirts warming by the stove." Carrie grabbed the toasty flannel shirts and followed the men into the bedroom. "I'll get the boys tucked in. There's hot coffee and pea soup on the stove."

Will and Tim were wide awake by the time she had them ready for bed, so she ladled out steaming bowls of soup for them. Then she joined her father and Matt, who sat at the kitchen table. "How did you find them?" she asked.

"It was Matt, really," Sam said. "He knew where the traps were, and he remembered a dense clump of oaks on a knoll right near one of the traps. Well, he was right. They'd huddled up under those trees for shelter."

"But why not head for home instead?"

"They got cut off, Carrie," Matt explained. "They'd rock-hopped across a creek, like they always did, but by the time they started back this way, a flash flood had swooshed down out of the hills, and that little creek was a torrent."

"Yup," Sam agreed. "It was a good thing they didn't try to get home. They'd have drowned for sure in that creek, the way it was roaring."

"Then how did you get to them?"

"It wasn't easy. Matt was just positive they'd be over on that hill, and when we hollered they hollered back. But with that flood between us, we were afraid they were stranded until morning. It was Harold that got across."

Carrie realized that her father and Matt had suddenly become very serious. "Is there something I don't know, Papa?"

"Harold figured he could swim the horses across, put the boys on the extra one, and swim them back."

It sounded reasonable to Carrie. "So, something went wrong? Someone was hurt? Eric?"

"Harold." Matt spoke softly. "I wanted to go. I know the country better, but he insisted he knew the horses better. He got across fine, put Will and Tim on one horse, and Eric in front of him on the other. When they were almost across his horse caught a leg in a tangle of brush and rolled over. Eric just sort of somersaulted over the horse's head onto firm ground."

"Harold's hurt bad, Carrie. He got pinned under the horse," Sam told her soberly.

"Where is he? Did you get him home?"

"A couple of Matt's friends were out looking. We waited for them. Then we rigged up a travois."

"A travois?"

"A sort of a stretcher that a horse can pull," Matt explained. "We took him home in that, and Bud went for the doctor."

"You said he was badly hurt, Matt. Is Anna alone with him? Papa, I should go to her."

"In the morning, Carrie. She isn't alone. We thought it best that we bring the boys home, but the Svensens are with Anna. And the doctor was on his way."

"Your father is right. You couldn't do anything there tonight. Perhaps he isn't as badly hurt as we thought. At any rate, the best thing for us to do is pray for him. Then I'll head back to the ranch, and you folks can get some rest."

When Matt left, the rain had stopped and a full moon was out.

The sky was cloudless the next morning. Sam and the boys dressed for meeting, but Carrie set out in the opposite direction. "You go and thank God for the boys' safety and pray for Mr. Arnesen. I'm going to help Anna."

"You're no nurse, Carrie. You'd be more help at prayer."

"No, Papa. If Mr. Arnesen is better, Anna will need someone to sit with him while she rests. If not . . . well, if not, she will need me then too."

Carrie was within sight of the Arnesen farm when she heard a horse behind her. She turned to see Matt reining in. "Want to ride the rest of the way?"

"No, thanks. I'm nearly there anyhow. Have you any news yet?"

"I talked to Bud this morning. He waited around for a while after he brought the doctor out." Matt's eyes avoided hers this time. "Doc said Harold was bleeding inside, from being crushed by the horse. It doesn't sound good."

He dismounted and walked on beside her, leading his horse. He tossed the reins over the porch rail as Eric came to the door. Eric's eyes were red, and his face was streaked with tears. Carrie wanted to reach out and hug him, but Matt threw a strong arm around the slumped shoulders. "Thought you might need help with the milking, Eric. And Miss Carrie came along to give your ma a hand."

"My pa's going to die, Mr. Hanlon." Eric sniffed and wriggled from Matt's embrace. "I went out in the rain and got lost, and now my pa's going to die, and it's all my fault."

71

"Nonsense, Eric. Your pa's going to be fine." Carrie looked down at the frightened face. "It was an accident, Eric. The storm wasn't your fault at all."

"She's right, Eric. I was there. I know just what happened, and it wasn't anyone's fault." Matt led Eric out to the barn, and Carrie pushed the door open and walked through the cold parlor and into the front bedroom.

Anna sat motionless beside the brass bed. Harold Arnesen's face was gray. His sunken eyes were fixed on his wife. At first Carrie thought he was gone, but then she heard him draw a single sharp gasp.

"Anna, Anna," she whispered. "It's me, Carrie. I came to see if I could do anything to help."

Mr. Arnesen gasped once again, and Anna laid a broad hand on his damp brow. Then she turned to Carrie. "Thank you for coming, Carrie. There is really nothing to be done. The doctor says all we can do is wait. Wait and pray."

"You look exhausted, Anna. You've been up all night, haven't you? Go and lie down for a few minutes."

"No, Carrie. I cannot leave."

"I will sit with him for a while, Anna. I'll call you if there is any change."

Anna quickly leaned over the bed, but Carrie had heard nothing. "Yes, Harold. What is it?" Carrie heard a soft moan and another of those awful, strangling gasps. Anna patted his shoulder and whispered, "No, Harold, I will not leave."

Anna raised her head, turned to Carrie, and spoke softly. "It will not be a long wait, Carrie. We have given each other a lifetime. We will give each other just a little longer."

Carrie went into the spotless kitchen. The stove fire had nearly gone out. She stirred the remaining embers and laid on some kindling. She brewed coffee for Anna and looked through the cupboard for something for the breakfast she was sure Eric hadn't eaten yet.

"Well, well, Eric," Matt said, as he and Eric came in from the barn. "It smells like Miss Carrie's stirred up some breakfast. Doesn't that sound good?"

"I'm really not hungry, Mr. Hanlon."

"How about pancakes, Eric?"

"No, thank you, Miss Carrie."

"I'll have some, Miss Carrie." Matt turned toward Eric. "And if you flip a couple of extras, I think I can persuade Eric to help get rid of them."

Eric had slipped into the bedroom.

"How is he?" Matt asked.

"Dying."

"And Anna?"

"Stunned, I think. She told me it wouldn't be long. I offered to sit with him so she could get a little rest, but she won't leave him, even for a moment."

"Would you, if it were your husband?"

His eyes were looking through her again, and she imagined herself sitting beside a dying husband with those same knowing eyes. She felt a little of what Anna must be feeling. "Of course I wouldn't."

Chapter Eight

Spring came slowly to the Salinas Valley that year. Rains came, intermittently, until mid-May, and warm sunny days started in March. The crops seemed determined to flourish; Matt Hanlon kept talking; and Carrie McLean kept trying not to listen to him.

Anna Arnesen grieved for her husband, comforted her son, and, as she told Carrie one warm afternoon, tried "to hang on one day at a time." When her friends saw her pick up her life and her tools, they quietly began to work beside her—Sam more often than the others.

Of course no one dared say anything to Sam, but Carrie smiled to herself, and Will and Tim snickered as they trudged down the road to Anna's farm one Saturday morning in early June. Sam had trimmed his mustache and slicked his gray-dusted sandy hair until it glistened.

"Now, boys," he called to his sons who were romping on ahead. "Settle down and don't wear yourselves out with racing. We're going to the Arnesens' to work, not so you can play with Eric."

"Work? Is that why you put on your good broadcloth shirt and spent a half-hour shaving?" Carrie asked with a smile.

"Now don't get sassy, Carrie," he replied. "You know I'm just being respectful."

"It's all right, Pa." Carrie nodded knowingly. "We're all fond of Anna, and we all admire the way she's trying to take care of herself and of Eric."

"She's such a plucky lady," Sam said. "And besides, we owe them, after what Harold did that night. He gave his life, he did, Carrie. It's the least we can do to help out his poor widow with her spring chores."

Will overheard the comment and sobered. "Pa, I swear, I'll never, never stay out in a storm like that again."

"Willie, we've been all over that." Carrie gave her brother a quick hug. "You made a mistake, but you must not blame yourself for what happened."

"It was my fault. I was the oldest and I should have gotten Tim and Eric home safe. If I had, Mr. Arnesen wouldn't have gotten killed."

"No one blames you, son," Sam assured him. "I think about it myself sometimes. If I'd been more careful with the horses, if I'd gone across with him. But we have to accept that it was his time. The Lord took him, Will."

"And don't either of you say anything to Eric about blame or fault," Carrie cautioned, remembering the little boy's anguish. "He's been feeling so bad about it as it is, and he has to get over his grief and go on with his life."

"And Mrs. Arnesen, too, that lovely lady." Sam nodded and picked up speed. "Takes a whole lot of courage to try to run a farm with no man around."

"Mr. Hanlon says she's the spunkiest lady he knows," Tim volunteered.

"Oh, he does, does he?"

"Jealous, Carrie?" Sam asked softly.

"Why should I be jealous, Papa? Now maybe you should be," she teased. "I do hear Mr. Hanlon's been spending almost as much time helping Anna as you have."

Sure enough, Matt's horse stood by the Arnesens' porch. Anna waved toward the pasture. "Matt's already out mending fences. Praise the Lord for him, and for you folks. Without your help . . ." She threw up hands whitened with flour. "But we're going to make it, Mr. McLean. Eric and I are going to be just fine."

Sam shooed Will and Tim toward a neat green and brown striped field. "Off, you two, and don't let me find a weed in those sugar beets by sundown." He grinned at Anna, whose black dress also showed a light dusting from her bread baking. "Wouldn't waste my time helping you if I didn't figure you'd make out okay."

"He comes for your bread, anyhow, Anna," Carrie told her. "I tried your recipe the other day, but it just doesn't come out the same for me."

"It's in the kneading, Carrie. Come on in the kitchen and watch how I do it. Sam, Matt did say he could use a stout hand with some fence rails, if you don't mind. Eric tries, but I do hate to see him struggle so hard to be a man."

Anna put her light, fat loaves in the oven. Home-made sauerkraut and sausages simmered on the stove for supper as she and Carrie shelled the first tender green peas from her kitchen garden.

"Oh, Carrie, I wish I knew how to thank you all. I know how much work you have at home, and your papa has done so much too. I do hope he isn't neglecting his own farm. Mr. Hanlon's come nearly every Saturday and Sunday afternoon too. He's a mighty fine young man, Carrie. Not many would give up so much of their free time to help an old widow."

"Maybe not an old one," Carrie laughed. "But you're certainly not old."

"For Matt?" Then it was Anna's turn to laugh. "Of course, maybe not for your papa now."

"So you have noticed?" Carrie teased.

"At first, of course, I didn't care to notice," she said softly. "But I've begun to suspect the clean shave and unfaded workclothes are not your idea. Do you think me shameless to mention it, Carrie? I did love Harold. I miss him terribly. Should missing him turn me from other men, Carrie, or to them?"

"I guess I never thought about it that way, Anna. Women marry; widows mourn; after a 'decent interval' they marry again. That's just the way it is, isn't it?"

"No, Carrie. It mustn't be like that. There must be love in a marriage for me, and for you."

"I hope so, Anna. I don't think I could marry without it." Carrie thought of Captain Stoneham. "Perhaps I won't marry at all. A girl doesn't have to, Anna. Not now.

There are other things, other ways for a single woman to live."

"I suppose so." Anna studied Carrie's deliberately expressionless face. "I hear there are girls in the city earning decent livings as switchboard operators, telegraphers, even in the shops. You've been a shop girl, haven't you?"

"Yes. I don't think I'd want to go back to that, though," Carrie told her. "The pay is low. It's all right if you live at home, but if you have to live in a boarding-house there isn't anything left over. Besides, I can't imagine years and years of standing there listening to the complaints. No, I've been thinking of learning to use a typewriting machine. I think I'd like working in an office."

"And living all alone?" Anna shook her head. "I can't imagine a girl like you spending a lifetime alone, and I don't think you will." Anna looked out the window and across the pasture to where Sam and Matt were working. "One of these days one of these young farmers will win your heart."

"Not likely, Anna," Carrie insisted.

The two women shelled peas in silence for a few minutes. Anna was obviously talking about Matt. *Does everyone notice how he hangs around all the time?* Carrie wondered. *But he never says anything about his feelings, well, nothing except how he is going to get rich farming. Doesn't he see that he doesn't have to be rich, just have enough, and sense enough to hold on to what he has?*

Carrie gazed out the window. If only he and Papa weren't so much alike. "Anna, you say there must be love in a marriage, but there must be more than that, I think. Mama loved Papa," she said slowly, then hesitated. "Maybe I shouldn't say this, Anna."

"If you want, Carrie. I am your friend. You can say anything you want to me."

"Mama loved Papa very much when they were married, but he promised her so much. He was a teamster and he was going to have his own cartage business. Then he was going to have his own truck farm, and sell produce in the city."

"So the cartage business didn't work out," Anna said gently. "He had some bad luck, but now he has his farm, and one of these days he'll probably have produce to sell in the city."

"Oh, Anna, you don't really believe that, do you? Why, it will take a miracle for him to even keep up the $100 a year payments on that land."

"Miracles have been known to happen."

"Not to people like us, Anna. People like us just keep drudging along, day after day, lucky to keep ourselves out of the poorhouse."

"Do you really have so little hope, Carrie? You are too young to have no dreams."

"You can't eat dreams," she said flatly. "That's what Mama always said. She believed in Papa's dreams, and so she married him. But the dreams didn't come true, and the love didn't last."

"Are you sure of that?"

Carrie thought a moment. She remembered exchanged looks over the dinner table, whispers, sounds in the night. "No," she admitted. "The love did last, I guess,

80

sometimes. But her life was so hard. She was so frail and tired."

"She was ill, Carrie. It is hard to keep hope when the body is sick. And it is natural to want an easier life for one's children. Of course she wanted that for you, just as I want this farm for Eric, not on shares, but free and clear, his own. Those are dreams, too, a mother's dreams."

Carrie's eyes filled. "She tried so hard, Anna."

"Then she had hope, Carrie," Anna declared. "And so, I think, do you. If you don't have hope, you quit. And you're not a quitter."

After supper Sam took Anna out to show her something about the new fence, and Matt asked Carrie if she had ever seen the valley at sunset from up in the foothills. It was a balmy spring evening, and the walk he suggested tempted her.

The hills were yellow with wild mustard. Bright orange poppies and deep lavender lupine nodded in the breeze. "Spring can be beautiful in the Salinas Valley, can't it?" Carrie mused.

Matt took her hand and helped her across a tiny stream. The rivulet still bubbled down the broad gully that had flown furiously a few months before. "I keep trying to tell you, Miss Carrie, it's a God-blessed place."

It did look blessed that evening, as the sun set behind the low line of clouds that capped the Santa Lucia Mountains. "All the flowers, Matt. I've never seen so many flowers. A few good rains, and it's like heaven."

"And look at the farms, Carrie, the crops. Why even the padres' old apple trees promise a bumper crop this year."

"This year, yes, when there's been rain." She remembered also how the same fields had looked the fall before, when she'd first seen them, when the cattle were starving on the hillsides. "But what about next year?"

"By next year it won't matter. By next year there will be dozens of deep wells all up and down the valley."

His cool blue eyes really saw the valley that way, Carrie realized. He already saw the tall white towers topped with whirling windmills and full water tanks. And as he looked at the fields green with spring's flourishing wheat, and with the lush alfalfa and sugar beets, he really believed that this same spring promise would be repeated year after year.

"There's only one well, Mr. Hanlon, on your boss's big ranch. The rest of us, even if we could be sure of striking water, could never pay the cost of such wells."

"Yes, we could, Miss Carrie. We are sure about the water. We've ample proof of it. And as for the cost, if we all work together, groups of farmers, pooling their efforts, we just might—"

"We?" Carrie interrupted. "It's easy for you to tell everybody what to do. It isn't your land, or your money." As soon as the words were out, she wished she hadn't said them.

"But it will be," he insisted. "I've got some savings already. I'm putting down some roots, making friends. The good Lord found me here, and here's where I belong." He took her hands in his, then, and looked into her face. He started to speak again, and she guessed that he saw her in that future. "We just . . ."

He bit his lower lip as if to stop the words and loosed his grasp on her hands. "The Lord has promised the fruitful plain to his people."

"You must remember you are a new Christian, Mr. Hanlon. Surely you can see that many of God's people suffer in this world. Those promises are for the future, for heaven. Here on earth we're on our own."

"Carrie, stop talking like that. You don't live that way. You work, hard. And you know, deep down, that it's worth it. People with no hope don't keep trying."

"No," she protested. "Papa works because he has hopes for his sons; Anna works because she has hopes for Eric; I work because I don't have any choice."

"That's not true, and you know it. I watched you pour dish water on cabbage seedlings last fall when nobody else bothered. I know you've cut up your own nice clothes to make shirts for your brothers. And I know how much time you spend here helping Anna with her chores after you've worn yourself out doing your own."

"But that's just simple decency," she insisted. "That doesn't mean I expect God to do me any favors." She hadn't realized that anyone, let alone Matt, had noticed the little things that seemed so commonplace to her. "It doesn't work that way. I know. Lots of people who are a lot better than me don't ever get their rewards."

He looked at her and it was as if he were struggling to pour into her his own faith. "It's true I haven't had a lot of schooling or have even heard the Word preached all my life as you have, Miss Carrie. But I believe what it says. The Bible says God will supply all our needs; it says he will reward our labor; it says whatever we do, as long as we follow his leading, he will bless it."

"Then most of his people must do a pretty bad job of following his leading, because most of the Christians I know have all they can do to keep food on the table."

"Maybe they work too hard at it."

"Too hard? Now what in the world do you mean by that, Mr. Hanlon?"

He thought a while before he answered. "I'm not real sure. I guess I mean they put their efforts into finding the food, instead of into finding the Lord's path."

"And how do you propose they find the Lord's path, then?"

"He called Abraham. He spoke to the prophets."

"Well, I don't know anyone who has visions in this day and age, and when people hear voices we put them in asylums," Carrie retorted.

"I don't know about visions, or about actually hearing voices for that matter. But, Miss Carrie, I know, as surely as I'm standing here looking at you, seeing your lovely face, hearing your doubts, sensing your longings, that the Lord has planted us in this valley just like he planted those willow trees. He's given us roots like they've got, and he wants us to be strong, like they are. And he intends that we and this valley will prosper together."

"I wish I could believe Papa when he talks like that, Mr. Hanlon, and I wish I could believe you. But Papa's dreams have failed so often." She looked out over the thriving acres, not daring to believe the promise they held. "Mr. Hanlon, this is not heaven. This is the real world, and lives cannot be built on dreams."

Carrie sighed and turned from his gaze, but Matt turned her face back to his own. "Not dreams, Miss Carrie. Not dreams, but faith. God has promised. Perhaps I am wrong on the details." He looked into her eyes again, then nodded slowly, as if the look had confirmed his vision.

Carrie looked across the green acres, but she wouldn't let herself believe their promise, or Matt's either. "I hope you're right, Mr. Hanlon, but I'm afraid I won't believe in Papa's dream until he's made that last payment on his land. And I won't trust your dreams until you've got the deed to your farm in your hands."

"You're wrong, Carrie, and one day I'll hand you that deed to prove it. God has promised we shall prosper here, and to God be the glory."

Chapter Nine

Thanks to the heavy winter rains there was water in most of the creeks into early September. The Salinas was still a river, not just a crack in the adobe floor of the valley.

That meant, of course, that the labor of the farm, while rewarding, was unrelenting. Everyone carried water from dawn to dusk for the long rows of sugar beets, corn, and vegetables. But they grew, and it was a joy to see the tender shoots poke through the soil, grow into the morning mists, and climb toward the afternoon sun.

The McLeans' rabbit and chicken stews had been bright with carrots, turnips, and snap beans for months already, and next week the real harvest season would begin. There would be potatoes, huge squashes, and bushels of carrots for the cellar Sam had dug under the front porch. There was plenty of corn for the chickens, and the stalks would be stored for the cow Sam planned to buy with the cash they had been promised from the sugar mill.

Mr. Hanlon came to call often in the long, mild evenings. He said he came to talk crops with Sam, but Sam, as often as not, had gone to Anna Arnesen's place "to lend a hand with the chores." Carrie knew her father was merely waiting a decent interval before asking for her hand.

As for Mr. Hanlon, he didn't appear to mind Sam's absences. Carrie pointed out that the neighbors would doubtless talk, but he laughed and reminded her that there were no neighbors to talk.

Will and Tim were delighted when he called, and it was no wonder. Carrie really couldn't send them to bed until he left, so they would sit on the porch steps listening to his tall stories until all hours.

". . . horses looked like little mice."

"Just imagine, Carrie! Flying!"

"Just imagine, Will. That's the closest you'll ever get to flying like a bird. Dirigibles! Big balloons you can ride in. Ha!"

"Miss Carrie, don't you ever believe in anything you haven't seen?" Matt laughed. "I guess I'll have to take you on a dirigible ride on our honeymoon."

Matt's eyes twinkled, but Carrie was never sure, when he looked at her like that, if he were serious, or only teasing her just as he teased the boys. After all, if he had any serious intentions, why hadn't he spoken of them? "Mr. Hanlon, I'm not certain which is more unlikely, the dirigible or the honeymoon."

He acted as if he hadn't heard her. "Will, Tim, I'll take you fishing in the morning if you can find some worms."

Carrie felt uncomfortable as the boys dashed off, leaving her and Matt alone on the dark porch. "Where do you expect to find any fish this time of year?" she asked quietly.

"Who knows? There's still some water in the river." He grinned and edged his chair a little closer to hers. "So you don't believe in honeymoons, Miss Carrie."

"Mr. Hanlon!" The boldness of the man! She tried to sound properly shocked, but how could she, when he sat there grinning like a schoolboy? "I really don't think honeymoons are a proper topic."

"But you aren't interested in airships."

"Airships are just like you. Way up in the air, out of reach, like all the notions you put in the boys' heads. Will and Timmy will be very lucky to have steady jobs or ten-acre farms when they grow up. Yet you sit here and talk about airships and motor cars. You tell them about cities like New York and Chicago, when they may never even see San Francisco again."

Carrie thought about Rob, on his way to the Philippines with the army. "Do you want to encourage them to go off to war too? Mr. Hanlon, their lives and our lives are here hauling water, plowing this hard clay, hoping to harvest enough food to last the winter and enough sugar beets to make the mortgage payment."

"Ah, then you do hope, Miss Carrie. Though you claim to expect nothing you don't have in your hand, you admit to hoping."

"Oh, don't be silly. It's a manner of speaking. Besides, I hope only for what I've earned."

"Why, of course. So do I. I'm earning my farm." He looked out across the fields of grain wafting in the moonlight, and his voice was intense when he spoke again. "I'm earning my farm, Miss Carrie, and I will have it. If I must have the deed in hand before you believe that, then I will bring you that deed."

Carrie was glad the darkness hid her face, for her cheeks burned.

Then he stood, and his tone was light again. "Too bad you can't dream with me, though. Honeymoons are no fun to plan alone."

Carrie rose, too, as he picked up his hat and started down the steps. Her forgotten knitting fell from her lap. Was it only an accident that, as they knelt together to gather it, his hand found hers? Was it only an accident that his long, soft mustache brushed her cheek?

Her real problem, Carrie knew, was the white hot excitement that filled her when it happened. *I can't go on like this*, she told herself. *I don't want to feel this way, not about Matt.* If only he would declare himself outright. No, she didn't want that either. With that offhanded arrogance of his he just might talk her into a promise she'd regret later. No, she simply had to avoid him, she decided, but how?

"Anna," Carrie confided a few days later, "Mr. Hanlon's been very nice to our family. Papa likes him; the boys adore him. How can I persuade him that he must not call when Papa isn't at home?"

"Does it really matter?"

"Of course, it matters. It isn't proper."

"Oh, it isn't?" Anna's pale blue eyes twinkled. "Doesn't sound to me as if he's taken any liberties."

"Well, not really. But it is so obvious what he's thinking. Anna, a gentleman doesn't talk to a lady about—about honeymoons!"

"Unless he plans on sharing one with her."

"That's exactly what I mean," Carrie argued.

"Now, Carrie, you don't have to be coy with me. You know as well as I do that Matt Hanlon's courting you."

"But I don't want Matt Hanlon to court me," Carrie insisted. "I've given him no encouragement."

"Hand me that cheesecloth, Carrie, so I can strain this vinegar." Anna nodded knowingly as she poured the hot, spicy vinegar over the crock full of sliced cucumber. "No encouragement. You just pass off these little accidental encounters and think he doesn't notice? You think he doesn't know you are as attracted to him as he is to you?"

"I am not, Anna." Carrie tried as hard to convince herself as to convince Anna. "How could you think I would want him to . . . to . . . ."

"Make advances? You don't really believe those fairy tales about ladies not having any feelings, do you?"

"Not for Matt Hanlon."

"And your face is red as a beet from the pickling. Carrie, he's a fine young man. He's hard working, smart, a good Christian."

"He's a farmhand. He's got a world of big ideas and no prospects whatsoever."

"As you frequently remind him." Anna's rebuke was so soft Carrie barely heard it.

"Somebody has to be realistic," she protested. "He's likely as not to take that little bit of savings he says he has, throw it away on a piece of worthless land, and lose it all."

"Sure, Carrie, he might lose it," Anna admitted. "Or he just might make a go of it, especially if he has some help."

"I suppose you mean my help." Carrie bit a trembling lip. "Mama helped Papa, until it killed her."

"But she was in love with him, Carrie. And you're in love with Matt."

"Maybe I do have some feelings for him, but at least I know enough to keep them under control. I'm not going to let some wild dreamer sweep me off my feet with stories about honeymoons in dirigibles."

That year the Fort Romie colony hosted a real harvest festival. Her pickles were not ready in time, but Carrie was proud of the tangy green tomato mincemeat she had made with Anna's help. She set her pies among the pumpkin and apple pies on the heavily laden tables.

Sam looked over the length of the table. The faces had become so familiar and loved in the past year. "But so many are missing," he mused. "I pray those who gave up during the hard winter have fared as well as have we who persisted."

Carrie had to admit their lives were better than she could remember. "It's been hard," she said. "Some of them just couldn't take it. They didn't know how, or they didn't have the strength or the savings to tide them over to harvest."

"You were ready once to join them. How about now, Carrie? Do you wish you were back in the city?"

"Sometimes, Pa." She couldn't lie to him. "Sometimes, when I ache all over and I'm sunburned and my hands are blistered."

"I'm sorry for that, daughter. I know it hasn't been easy, but we've plenty. For the first time since I lost my team when you were just a little tyke, we've a stake. We have a house of our own and land. We've food—bushels of potatoes and carrots and shelves full of preserves. There's a little money laid by, even."

She was forced to agree. "We've done well, Pa."

"We've had help, of course, from Matt and the Arnesens and the Salvation Army, God bless them, and the Almighty himself most of all."

"Yes. Thank God for the good weather this year. I just pray it continues."

"Won't really matter in another year or two, with all the wells going in," he offered.

"Maybe," she admitted. Matt did seem to have been right about the wells. They were being drilled on most of the bigger ranches. The whirring blades of the windmills and the big redwood water towers were becoming familiar sights. "By the way, where's Mr. Hanlon been? I haven't seen him for several days."

Sam hesitated, and Will piped in. "He went to Salinas City, Carrie. He said he'd be back for the festival, though. He said he wouldn't miss the festival or Carrie's mince pies for anything."

"He said to save him a piece." Tim started to slip a second piece of pie onto his own plate.

"Did not." Will pushed the pie away from his brother. "You're sneaking that for yourself." He turned to Carrie. "Matt said he'd be on the two o'clock train and he'd be here before three."

"That's enough, boys," Sam interrupted. "He also said not to tell Carrie where he was going."

"Why in the world not, Pa? Why should I care if Matt Hanlon goes to Salinas City for a few days?" But Carrie felt her heart flutter. *Why, indeed?* she asked herself. *But what if he didn't come back?* "So what?" She shrugged. "He can go for good if he likes. It's none of my business."

The rich pie lost its tang. Even the flattering comments about it lost their savor, until she saw Matt striding across the field to the cluster of oaks where Carrie sat with her family. Tim handed him the slice of pie he really had saved.

"Wow! I told you I wouldn't miss Carrie's mince pie. Miss Carrie, you've outdone yourself."

"Sorry you've missed the rest of dinner, Mr. Hanlon."

"So am I, but trains can't be rushed."

"Will said you went to Salinas City. Did you have a good trip?"

Matt shot a look at Will. "I had some business there. I guess you could say it went well. I got what I went for, anyhow."

"Come on, Matt." Will shoved the now empty pie plate away, and Tim tugged at Matt's sleeve. "Come on. There's still time for a baseball game before dark."

Carrie helped the other women clear away the feast while the boys, big and little, played their ball game. When dusk came, they hushed the youngsters and gathered for a prayer of thanksgiving. Carrie puzzled as Matt, after thanking God for bringing the Salvation Army and the gospel to him, asked for blessing "in our new venture together."

"May I please walk you home, Miss Carrie?" he asked, as the McLeans started down the lane.

He sounded so serious that she was almost afraid to answer. Was this the time? Would he speak to her now and ask for a promise? "Of course, you may walk along with us, Mr. Hanlon."

"Alone?"

"Papa?" *Please let him say no,* she thought.

"It's all right, Carrie. The boys and I will go on ahead and see you at the house in a little while."

"Yes, Papa. I'll be along in just a few minutes." Men! Couldn't her father see that she wanted an excuse? *Well, let Matt ask if he wants to. I don't have to let him talk me into anything.*

"Miss Carrie, I didn't want the boys to tell you about my going to Salinas, because I wanted to tell you myself."

"Is something wrong, Mr. Hanlon?"

"Not really. No, not at all. Carrie, I'm leaving Soledad for a while."

"Oh!" She felt the thud physically. It was as if he'd kicked her in the stomach. "You're leaving the valley, Matt? But your plans, your dreams?"

"That's why I'm going, Carrie. I'm going to work at the sugar mill."

"I can't believe you've given up." Why did she have to protest? *Why not just let him go, and not be bothered anymore by him?* she wondered.

"I've not given up, Miss Carrie. I will have my farm, for the good Lord has promised it to me. But I'm an impatient man. I cannot wait forever. So I am going to work at the mill to make more money. I'll be able to save two, maybe three dollars a week from my pay there."

The amount surprised her. "So much. Wages must be very good."

"The harvest has been good, and the mill is going full blast. And living's cheap. There's a company boarding-house."

"I see." Carrie couldn't believe her calm response, when she trembled inside from head to toe. "Then you'll take your savings and move on to a good farming area."

"I'll be back, Miss Carrie. I'll be back when I've money for two things—a down payment and a deep well."

"I do wish you well, Mr. Hanlon." How cool she sounded, but how cold she felt. "We shall miss you."

"Miss Carrie." He took her hands in his and faced her. "Miss Carrie, I will be back. I'll buy that farm. And . . ." He looked at her, through her, again. "And something else too."

His eyes remained cool, but his hands were perspiring as he held hers. "Carrie, I know how you feel about my dreams. But when I do have that farm, I'll be dreaming still."

The full harvest moon was rising, and the breeze whispered in the willow trees along the creek bed. She waited for his question, believing with all her heart, at that moment, that he would be back soon to buy that farm.

His grasp on her hands loosened. "Well, Miss Carrie, I guess that's it."

That was all he said. Carrie took his offered arm, and they walked deliberately up the dusty road. She blinked back tears as she asked, "How soon are you leaving?"

"Tomorrow afternoon, after church. I'm leaving my horse with your pa and taking the train up. I start work Monday morning."

Chapter Ten

T isn't a real mountain."

"'Tis so, Eric Arnesen."

"Then where's the other half, smarty?"

"It's called Half Dome. The other half got cut off and carried away by a glacier. Mr. Hanlon!" Will shouted, though Matt and the other adults were only in the next room. "Mr. Hanlon, tell Eric about Half Dome."

"Excuse me a minute, folks." Matt stuck his head through the bedroom door. "Pictures don't lie, now, do they? So, Eric, there must be half a mountain." As he slid back into his chair his baffled look brought smiles to Sam and Anna. "Boys," he muttered. "I thought a stereopticon would keep them quiet and out of mischief."

"They love it, Mr. Hanlon. But they love bickering too." Matt's fingers brushed Carrie's as she handed him the dice. "It's your turn," she continued.

He tossed the dice and danced his piece across the Parcheesi board.

The cabin kitchen was warm with a good fire in the stove and good fellowship around the table. *Who better to join us*, Carrie reflected, *on this very special evening, but Anna and Matt?* Sam had still not proposed to Anna, but Carrie half expected he would before the night was over.

And Matt? Sam considered him a fourth son already. The evening would have been spoiled if he had not come down from Salinas City. If he should ask the question he almost asked two months ago, what would Carrie say? Would she have to be practical and reject the best he had to offer? She knew now he loved her. And Anna had been right about Carrie's feelings too. But Carrie was still sure that if she married for love alone, she, like her mother, would live to regret her folly.

"Wake up, Carrie. It's your turn, and you're about to beat us all."

"What?" Her father's words startled her. "Oh, I'm sorry. I was thinking." Her toss of the dice did finish the game. "Anyone for popcorn?" she asked, pushing back the chair.

"Me," came the chorus from the bedroom.

"Nobody asked you!" Matt laughed. "Nobody had to." He stood too. "Thinking about the new century, Carrie? It's almost here. Just a few hours."

"The twentieth century." She felt his breath on her neck as he reached past her to lift the heavy skillet down from its hook. "I suppose the days will go on just as they always have, but the very phrase seems so . . . so momentous, so exciting."

"So full of promise, Miss Carrie. The twentieth century. It's our century, Carrie. Yours and mine to mold and build."

"Don't you find a whole new century a little intimidating, Mr. Hanlon?" She laughed as she shook the golden kernels into the skillet. "But of course you're never intimidated."

"A century is just a lot of years. Plenty of time to plow and plant and harvest."

"Where's the popcorn?" They were suddenly invaded by small boys. "Oh, Papa, Mr. Hanlon's whispering to Carrie behind the stove."

"He doesn't care. 'Sides, Papa's whispering to Eric's mama," Will retorted.

"Nobody's whispering to anybody." Matt took the skillet from Carrie and shook it faster. "The popcorn's making too much noise, not to mention three small boys with big mouths."

"Golly, Mr. Hanlon, those stereopticon slides are just wonderful. Are there really places like that?" Eric asked.

"Sure," Will interrupted. "He's even been to that Yosemite place, haven't you, Mr. Hanlon?"

"He's been just about every place there is."

"Not quite, Tim. I have been to the Yosemite Valley, though. But that is one place that is so big and so beautiful that even seeing isn't quite believing. I guess when God looked at the world he'd made and saw that it was good, maybe he was looking especially at places like that."

Carrie set a mixing bowl on the top of the stove, and Matt tipped the skilletful of steaming popcorn into it and handed it to Eric. "Take that and back to the bedroom with you."

"Okay, Mr. Hanlon. I want to see the picture of the half-mountain again."

"Once more, Eric. But don't wear it out," Will warned. "Mr. Hanlon gave it to Timmy and me, after all."

"They do love your Christmas gift, Matt. We all thank you for your generosity," Sam said, turning from his conversation with Anna as Carrie set a second bowl of popcorn on the kitchen table.

"Yes, Mr. Hanlon," Carrie agreed. "But you shouldn't have spent so much, what with saving for your farm."

"Do you mind the delay so much, Miss Carrie?"

Those eyes again! No matter what she said, he read something more into it. "It's just that I know how anxious you are to have your own farm. And you'll never have it if you throw your money away on expensive gifts."

"If it's a comfort to you, I made a little extra fixing some machinery." He smiled at her. "My plans are right on schedule."

"Have you a special piece of land in mind, Matt?" Anna inquired.

"Not really, Mrs. Arnesen. But a couple of the plots that have been abandoned here at Fort Romie are good pieces."

"Surely not, Mr. Hanlon. There's no water here in a dry year. Wouldn't something closer to the river be better?" Carrie asked. "Surely you know better than to tackle land that has already proved unfarmable."

"One more year like this one, Carrie, and we'll have enough money between us—me, Matt, a couple other families—to dig a well." Sam was talking to Carrie, but his look was for Anna. "Then we'll have good, productive land for our wives and children."

Anna's eyes dropped to the table, but her hand met Sam's as they both reached toward the popcorn bowl. *So that is why he hasn't asked her yet*, Carrie realized. *He does know it takes more than dreams.* It scarcely occurred to her that Matt was holding back for the same reason.

"How long is it to the new century?" a sleepy voice called from the bedroom.

"I told you, you wouldn't be able to stay awake that long."

"Yes, we can, Carrie." Tim and Eric were rubbing their heavy eyes as Carrie looked into the bedroom, but Will was determined to stay awake until midnight. "They're just little kids, but I'm not sleepy. Please, Carrie, may I come and wait up with you and Papa?"

"It's all right, Carrie. This is the only century he'll have a chance to see in, after all." Sam tucked the quilt around Tim and Eric, who had given up the struggle and slept. "It's just past eleven now."

"We've been talking plans, Will." Matt poured a cup of tea for the boy, despite Carrie's frown. "What do you think the new century has in store for us?"

Will looked around the table. "Gosh, I just hope it's as good as the past year has been. 'Cept for Mr. Arnesen, ma'am. I mean, like this. Us all together and lots to eat and no landlord pestering for the rent and Carrie not having to go to work in the shop."

Carrie saw the surprise on her father's face. She, too, had not realized little Will was growing up. It was Matt who answered. "Will, you've found the secret of happiness. A family. I never had one." He looked around the little table. "'Til now, anyhow."

"When Robbie gets home it will be my turn," Will went on. "Then I'm going to go see the world, like you, Mr. Hanlon. And then I'm going to come right back here, and I'm going to have my own farm too."

"That's a good dream, Will," Sam said proudly. "Go and see. But come back home; take over the farm; find a good wife."

Will shook his head then, firmly. "No wife. Just Carrie, and Mrs. Arnesen I guess, but no girls."

And so the nineteenth century ended on a merry round of laughter as Sam counted off the last minutes on his pocket watch. "11:58, 11:59, 12:00 midnight, January 1, 1900." Sam swept Anna from her chair and into the air. "Happy New Year, Anna," he cried, obviously forgetting the gray in his hair.

If Matt happened to forget the proprieties just for a moment, Carrie thought, *well, how often does a new century begin?* But his was no spontaneous hug. His arms encircled her gently; his mouth found hers; and his caress lingered until they heard Anna and Papa hustle Willy off to bed.

As Sam and Anna whispered over the sleeping boys, Matt slowly released her. "I'm sorry, Miss Carrie. I guess I got carried away by the New Year and all. I shouldn't have done that."

But he wasn't sorry, she knew. And neither was she. There was no room now in her heart for fear or for doubt. With his strong arms around her she had felt, for the first time in her memory, completely safe. Matt's strength could protect her from anything.

He fumbled in his pocket and drew out a small box. "Carrie, maybe this isn't proper, either, but when I saw it in the Sears Roebuck catalog I knew you must have it."

He handed her the blue leather case. She struggled against the surge of yearning within her. "Mr. Hanlon, you know I can't accept a gift like this," she murmured, her hand trembling as she held it out to him.

"Please open it, Carrie. You can at least open it."

A pale blue satin lining cradled a delicate gold bow-knot clasp from which a tiny oval watch hung.

"Oh!" Carrie knew the gold was only plate. And she knew he could not afford even that. But Carrie had never owned anything so lovely. "Mr. Hanlon, it is the most beautiful gift I have ever received, but I simply cannot accept it." She repeated the words like the well-learned formula it was. "A lady . . ."

". . . must not accept jewelry from a gentleman," he finished. "Unless he is her father, her husband, or her betrothed."

Carrie's heart was still thumping from the ardor of his kiss. His grip on her hands was firm, possessive, yet protecting. His eyes, for once, looked only at her and not through her. "But Mr. Hanlon . . ."

"But nothing. Carrie, I know you love me."

She was too short of breath to even protest.

"I know you want me every bit as much as I want you."

Carrie was hot. She felt faint. Where were Papa and Anna? It wasn't proper to let him say such things. "Matt," she gasped. "Matt," she whispered, as he held her again.

"Carrie, you are right," he murmured into her ear. "I shouldn't say such things. I would be the happiest man alive if I could ask for your hand and receive a favorable answer. But I can't even ask that yet. I can only ask you to wait for me, Carrie. Wait, just a little while."

"Wait?" That was the last thing Carrie wanted to do then.

"Just a few more months, Carrie." His voice was still soft as he held her at arm's length. "Then I will be back here to stay. Will you keep the watch until then, Carrie, close to your heart? And keep me close to your heart too. Carrie, when I come back, when I bring you the deed to that farm then, may I ask you to be my wife?"

Her head whirled. His closeness stirred her as she had never been stirred before. She wanted him to hold her again, even to kiss her again. He had her heart, and if he had asked for her hand she'd have given him the pledge in an instant. But he'd only asked her to wait. "Matt, we don't know. So much can happen in the next months."

"I know you don't share my faith in the future, Carrie."

"But . . ."

She wanted to tell him that she did share his faith, but he put a finger to her lips. "I am not asking for your promise now, Carrie. I'm only asking for hope, for purpose in my planning. If it doesn't work out, if for some reason God doesn't bless my efforts, I will hold you to no promises."

"I love you, Matt Hanlon. I love you, and you have my promise now."

"I love you, Carrie McLean," he murmured, as his arms circled her body once more. "But I have made promises, both to myself and to you. I will not accept your promise until I have kept mine and have a home to bring you to."

Chapter Eleven

*C*arrie tucked the little watch away, not daring to hope that Matt's dreams, which were now her dreams, would really come true. The cabbages, carrots, and beets in her little kitchen garden sprouted in an unseasonably warm January sun, and the pastures glowed rich as emeralds.

It was early March before Matt was able to visit again, and by then prickles of doubt were creeping over the still sunny valley.

"No rain, Matt. Not a drop." Sam sighed, waving toward the sprouting potatoes and sugar beets. "The crops look fine now, still drawing dampness from the fall rains, but we've not had a drop of rain since Christmastime."

"We need that well, Sam. We could drill one for a hundred dollars, one fifty at most," Matt declared.

"I talked to the Brewsters and to Jack Morton," Sam told him. "That's about the only Fort Romie people left, and neither of them has any money laid by at all."

"I can come up with about fifty dollars."

"No, Matt. We can't take your money when you've no land to use the water. Anyhow, I've no more than that myself. We got a good bit for the sugar beets last fall, but with the payment on the land, and then I bought the cow. . . . Seemed like a good idea at the time."

"It was, Sam. That cow'll pay for herself in butter and cheese in a year, not to mention milk for yourselves. You're right," Matt conceded. "We can't raise the money by ourselves."

Matt and Sam sat opposite each other at the kitchen table, staring at the lush fields. Matt's eyes had avoided Carrie's ever since he arrived, and she knew why. Now she turned away from her cooking. "There's still time," she reminded them. "If we get good rains this month and next we'll do fine."

Matt smiled, then. "Now you're the one with the dream, Carrie. And you're right. The good Lord put us here. He will take care of us."

"Captain Burgess said just last week this was just a testing," she said. "I'm praying for rain, Matt, and trying to trust."

Matt turned back to Sam. "Any chance of the Salvation Army funding the well?"

"I did broach the subject, but the captain seemed doubtful. You know Mr. Jacks is the biggest landowner in the valley, and he says it's a lot of foolishness trying to irrigate."

"But Spreckles is doing it," Matt countered.

"Perhaps you should talk to the captain about it, Matt," Carrie suggested. "Since you work for Mr. Spreckles and have helped the drilling crews, maybe he would listen to you." She felt a pounding pulse at her throat. Just seeing Matt again reminded her of his arms around her on New Year's Eve. How she wanted his dreams to come true, all of them. "The captain isn't a farmer either, but he thinks a lot of you."

"That's a good idea, Carrie," Sam agreed. "Why don't you have a talk with the captain before you head back up to Salinas, Matt?"

Carrie had hoped for a few minutes alone with Matt, but he and Sam set out right after dinner to talk with Captain Burgess. Carrie and the boys met them at evening meeting, and she had to be content sitting next to him, trying to concentrate on the preaching.

"What happened?" Will demanded as soon as the benediction had been said.

"Shhh, Will. Not in church." But Sam hurried them outside and shared the news. "Captain Burgess can't spend that kind of money on his own authority, but he saw the wisdom of what we proposed and promised to present it to headquarters."

"That's wonderful news! Oh, Matt, if they would drill the well and let us pay the costs back from the crops . . ."

Carrie dared not say the rest of what she was thinking, but Matt was not so reserved. "Yes, Carrie. We could make it. I could buy one of the abandoned plots." He drew her apart from Sam and the boys. "And then I could ask you to wear your New Year's gift for all to see."

She felt almost ashamed of her doubts. "I'm sorry, Matt. It just seemed best to say nothing for the time being. That night, the excitement."

His hands squeezed hers sharply. "That wasn't all it was. Carrie, you haven't changed your mind? You couldn't."

"No," she admitted. "I haven't changed." The hot flush she felt on her cheeks proved that, if her words didn't. "I want just what you want, but we don't know, either of us, what the next months will bring. You did say 'no promises,' Matt."

"All right. No promises." The other worshipers were drifting out of the building. Matt held her hands a few more moments, and his breath caressed her as his lips could not. "No promises, for now."

Matt came back to Soledad in June, but it was not to buy his farm or to ask for Carrie's hand. The sugar mill had closed, and he was out of a job. Last year's beet crop was all processed, and it was obvious there would be no sugar beets in the Salinas Valley this year.

He and Sam had just rinsed their grimy hands in the pan of mud-tinged water by the sink. "Too late, Sam. We needed well water months ago. And deep, drilled wells, not another shallow hole in a muddy riverbed."

"It was the money, Matt." Sam sighed. "The Army just didn't have money to lend us for a drilling crew and equipment. Times are hard all over. They have so many needy people to help. So we dug the best we could."

"Just you and Burgess?"

"Jack Morton helped us with the digging."

"I thought they'd pulled out," Matt said.

"They did." Carrie's words were bitter. She'd let herself hope, and hope had betrayed her again. "When the well came in so muddy and foul, Mrs. Morton told Mr. Morton she was leaving and he could do as he pleased."

"Carrie's said almost the same to me, Matt, and I can't say as I blame her."

"But where would you go if you did give up?" Matt asked.

"I don't know," Sam answered. "Sometimes I think that's the only reason we're still here. Everything I have is here, and all I can do is trust the good Lord not to take it from me. Besides, we're not that likely to starve. The water's foul, but it keeps the vegetable garden growing. With straining it's almost fit for us and the cow and the chickens. There's nothing green out there for them to eat, but they can scratch up something."

"So far," Carrie put in. "The cow's drying up already."

"But she's due to calve in a few weeks," Sam explained. "Once the calf is weaned we'll have milk as long as she can find any pasture at all."

"Yes, Sam, and veal too," Matt reminded him.

"Matt," Carrie asked, "is the water we have, bad as it is, at least likely to last all summer?"

"Probably, Miss Carrie. It won't be easy, hauling it from the riverbed, but you'll make it fine, and next year there'll be rain again."

"Always the optimist." Her eyes met her father's, and she knew that he, too, was thinking about the mortgage payment. But there was no need to remind Matt that without a cash crop this year, there would be no next year to look forward to. "I suppose that means you're staying on," she continued. "At least you should be able to buy a farm dirt cheap right now."

109

He actually smiled at her. "I've been thinking the same thing myself, Miss Carrie. I've got my eye on a piece just north of here, but it's part of the Fort Romie parcel, and the Salvation Army still hasn't decided if it wants to sell."

"Perhaps you should hold off, Matt. There's not likely to be any farm work for several months, and you might need your savings to tide you over." Sam's uncharacteristically cautious words surprised Carrie.

"Not if I can possibly help it. I've got other plans for that nest egg, Sam."

The words were addressed to her father, but Matt looked at Carrie. She sensed that he wanted reassurance, but she had none to give. "Matt, the way this valley looks now you may well find those savings the only thing between you and the poorhouse. You can't eat your lovely plans."

"I'll manage, Miss Carrie, just as you and your pa will manage. But, God willing, I'll not touch a cent of our farm money for living expenses."

If Sam heard the reference to "our" farm, he didn't mention it. "Thanks for the help hauling the water, Matt. You'll stay for supper, of course."

"As a matter of fact, Sam, I have to be on my way. The boss of one of the drilling crews has been staying at the boardinghouse for the weekend, and I want to talk to him about a job."

"Oh, I see." Sam bit his lip and mumbled something. "You don't have time to stop off at the Arnesens', then?"

"I guess I could for a minute. Why?"

"Well, I haven't checked things over there lately. I'd just like to make sure everything's all right."

"I'd be glad to look in on Anna, Sam, but I thought that was something you were taking care of yourself," Matt teased.

Sam kicked at the edge of the rag rug. "I guess I was, but the way things are now . . ." He looked at Carrie and then at Matt. "You know how it is. I had plans too. I guess it's no secret. I know she's expecting me to come courting, but what can I say to her when I've nothing to offer."

Matt nodded grimly. "But, Sam, she'll be wondering why you're avoiding her."

"That's right, Papa," Carrie added. "It's been weeks since you've been over there. Anna even mentioned it at the sewing circle."

"Maybe. But Anna's a good catch. She should be setting her cap for someone who can make a good life for her and her boy," Sam said glumly.

"Tell you what, Sam," Matt offered. "I'll turn down your request for now. You just go over and pay that call yourself. Anna Arnesen knows this country. She doesn't expect things to be easy."

"She's told me about the hard times she and Mr. Arnesen had when they first came here, Papa, and she doesn't seem to regret it." Carrie tried to encourage her father and maybe herself too.

"That's no excuse for me to offer more of the same, Carrie. Even with your mother, young as we were, we had hope; we had a future."

"Sam McLean, you still have hope and a future." Matt shook a determined finger at Sam. "I've put a lot of effort into making a farmer out of you, and I'd hate to see it go to waste." He laughed, then, and Sam laughed with him.

"All right, Matt. I'll go see Anna tonight, right after supper."

"Good. Then I'll be on my way and see you folks at Sunday meeting."

Carrie went out on the porch, too, to call Will and Tim in for supper, and Matt took her arm as they went down the steps.

"Carrie, don't give up," he begged. "I meant that about not spending our money. Even if the job with the drillers doesn't come off, I'll find some kind of work, and as soon as the Salvation Army decides on new terms I'll buy."

"You know, with your determination, I almost believe you will."

"Only 'almost'?"

"It is going to be a long time before we see another decent harvest, Matt." The doubts crowded back into Carrie's mind and heart. "How can you believe we'll still be here then? You will, maybe, but Pa is going to lose this place in September, when the mortgage payment comes due."

"No, he isn't, Carrie."

"He'd never take money from you, if that's what you're thinking."

"Probably not," Matt conceded. "But somehow he'll come up with that mortgage payment."

"Another one of your 'promises'?"

"Yeah, I guess so. But, Carrie, I know."

When he was with her, when he looked at her and into the future, Carrie almost believed him. But all summer long the sun beat down on the baked adobe soil of the valley. Matt found work, but it took him away from Soledad. His visits became rare, and each blistering day his dreams became more unreal to Carrie, like mirages on the dusty roads.

The hot east wind was normal for September. *At least this year it's not hurting the crops,* Carrie told herself. *Everything's already dead.*

She saw Sam trudging up the road, still leading the bawling calf he'd gone to town to sell. "Nobody's buying, Pa?" she asked, before she saw the grin he wore. "Pa, you obviously have some good news, even if you do still have the calf."

"Oh, that. Well, it's still hot for butchering, but I didn't try, anyhow. I stopped at the post office, and there was a letter from Rob."

"What could Rob have had to say that would stop you from trying to get a few more dollars toward the mortgage payment, Papa?"

"Not what he said as much as what he sent. Carrie, Rob sent a money order for one hundred dollars!"

"A hundred dollars! Papa, where would Robbie get that much money?"

"Says he's been saving it for a stake when he gets out of the army."

"Then it's his money, and he wants you to bank it for him."

"That's what I thought, too, but he says he's decided to stay in the army for now. He's been promoted to corporal and will probably make sergeant in a few months."

"It's still his money."

"But like he says, he doesn't need it right now. And he says in his letter 'Invest it in the farm. You can pay me back from the profits.'"

"What profits?" Carrie snorted. "Invest in this?" She kicked the soil, but the adobe was baked so hard she didn't even raise dust.

"Carrie, I've prayed to the Lord that, if it was his will for us to stay here, he would provide the mortgage money, and here it is. Rob's money order is a direct answer to prayer."

"But whose prayer, Pa?"

"Now what do you mean by that?" he asked.

The searing wind drove a tumbleweed between them. "Maybe I've been saying some prayers of my own," Carrie told him. "Pa, with that money we could get out of here."

He looked as if he couldn't believe what he had heard. "Get out? Abandon the money we've already spent, two years of hard work? Just walk away?"

"Abandon two years of blisters and failure? Yes."

"And where would we go, Carrie? Back to San Francisco?"

"Why not?" she asked defiantly.

"And shut your little brothers up in a flat, with no sunshine or fresh air? I suppose you'll tell me you want to go back to selling gloves at the Emporium."

"It wasn't so bad." *Well*, she told herself, *it wasn't that bad.*

"And what about me?" Sam demanded. "A man has his pride. Do you want me to go back to pounding the streets begging for a few hours' work?"

"With a hundred dollars you could buy your own team and wagon, or a hack even," she insisted.

"Not with the expenses of moving back, and we would need money to live on until we got settled."

"We could manage, Pa."

"No, Carrie. At least we haven't gone hungry here. And here, we have a future. We have something that is ours, something that will last. Carrie, have you no feel at all for the land?"

"Not for this land," she snapped. "This worthless, unrewarding land. What good is it to have land that produces crops once in three years, if we're lucky?"

"You know it will produce every year, if we can just get the water," he persisted.

"You and Matt, and your precious wells."

Her father looked at her, hard, and lowered his angry voice. "What about Matt, Carrie? Even if I could give up the land, I couldn't take you back to San Francisco. You belong here, with Matt."

"Whatever makes you think so?" Carrie recalled Matt's assurance to her that there was no promise between them, even when she'd offered him that promise. "In fact, he seems to be avoiding me." Her voice was bitter as she reminded her father that Matt had hardly been around that summer.

"When could he come, traipsing up and down the valley with that well-drilling crew?"

"As little money as there is around here, I doubt he's been working that steady," Carrie grumbled.

"He hasn't been doing so bad, but you know he's been on the road a lot."

"Well, he's perfectly free to keep on traipsing." Carrie shrugged for her father's benefit though her heart ached. "We have no understanding of any kind at all."

"None?" Sam pursed his lips and nodded. "I admit he hasn't asked me for your hand, but I was pretty sure it was only a matter of time."

"How much time?" she muttered. "Does he expect me to wait forever?"

"You are getting on in years, aren't you?" Sam attempted a teasing grin. "Nearly twenty. I think you've a little time before we hang the spinster label on you."

"Oh, Papa."

"So, do you want to go back to the city to look for a better suitor?"

"No." Carrie hadn't meant to say it quite that sharply. "No, Pa. I want to go back to the city because I can't see any future here for any of us. Next year, where will the mortgage payment come from?"

"Next year there will be rain."

"Sure. The Lord promised it, I suppose."

"A little faith never hurts," Sam reminded her. "God has helped us out more than once before."

"You can't eat faith."

"Carrie, what do you think we've been eating the past two years, if not faith?"

"Sweat!" She almost spat out the word.

"Oh, Carrie." He looked away from her angry face. "I know it's been hard for you, terribly hard. But surely you can see that God has been with us. The Lord gave us this land and the good harvests last year." Sam nodded firmly. "It is good land, and now the Lord has given me the money to keep it."

Chapter Twelve

*S*am left early the next morning, Rob's money order safe in his pocket. "I'm taking this over to Captain Burgess right away, Carrie, before anything else can happen. We are going to hold on to this place, praise the Lord."

"The Lord and Rob. Papa, have you thought at all about what I said yesterday?"

"Of course I have, Carrie, but it isn't right. We can't go backward."

He strode down the dusty road, and Carrie ladled a bucket of water out of the barrel. The barrel was less than a quarter full, and she had to be very careful not to stir up the mud that had settled to the bottom. No point in putting more mud on the floor than she scrubbed off. "Men! Men, and their fool hunger for land." She jabbed the mop under the stove. "If they want dirt, they should try keeping house for a while."

Carrie lugged the scrub bucket outside and carefully emptied it around the straggly cornstalks. "Here's your precious water," she muttered. "Hope you don't mind that I used it first to mop the kitchen floor." There were several ears on each stalk, and the silks were beginning to fade. "At least we'll have sweet corn for Sunday dinner."

Carrie heard the clatter behind her. The water wagon was early, and it sounded like Billy was in an awful hurry. "Miss Carrie?" he called. "Miss Carrie, is your pa around?"

"He had an errand with Captain Burgess, Billy. I'll give you a hand with the water barrel."

"Oh, sure. That ain't the problem. Miss Carrie, there's wildfire across the river."

Her eyes followed his outstretched arm. She wondered that she hadn't noticed before. A thick plume of smoke billowed just south of Soledad and stretched along the midline of the hills to the east of the valley. "Is it bad, Billy? Are homes in danger?"

"Any fire's trouble this time of year. Everything's so tinder dry it just eats up the land. Miss Carrie, I'm on my way to the Burgesses', but if I should miss your pa, tell him we need every pair of hands on the fireline. We've got to stop it at the river or it could take the whole valley."

As he hurried off, Carrie watched the smoke. She hadn't thought the east wind could be any hotter than the past week, but now it carried the heat of both sun and fire. As she picked a few withered apples from the old trees, she looked across the valley. The smoke was heavier. It lay thickly now, blotting out the Gabilan Ridge entirely. Her eyes were beginning to smart, though the fire was still three or four miles away.

118

Sam had met Billy on the road, and he stopped to tell Carrie that he and Will were on their way to help. He'd drop Timmy off at the Arnesens, he said.

Anna! Carrie thought. Anna's rented farm was just across the river, south of town. *Right there*, she pictured, *just in front of the rising black cloud.*

It was too hot to work. *There must be something I can do to help*, she thought, *but Papa had said to stay here.* She went into the house, but she couldn't leave the window. It was as if she were mesmerized by the ever-darkening overcast. She thought she could even see, now and then, tongues of orange flame at the base of the blackness.

"Oh, Lord," Carrie found herself crying, in her fear. "Lord, if you do care anything about us, spare us any more trouble. Please, Lord, no more. Don't let Anna be burned out. You've already taken her husband and kept Pa so poor he won't propose to her. Don't take her farm too."

Carrie went outside, but the smoke and the tears it brought to her eyes prevented her from seeing even the line of willows that marked the riverbed. "The river." She snorted. "Some river. It's so dry that the fire will burn right across it." She shuddered. "If it does we'll lose everything, even the payment Papa just made. No! No! No!" No god could be that cruel. "God, Papa trusts you. You can't take his dream away from him. You can't."

Carrie wasn't imagining it now. She could see the red glow that turned to black as it rose in the air. It stretched for three or four miles where she knew the river must be. And Sam and the boys were out there with shovels trying to stop it. "Oh, God." Now she was pleading. "Oh, God,

119

watch over them, and keep them safe from the fire, please."

Carrie couldn't help herself. She stood at the window and stared at the terrible scene for hours. The worst part was not knowing. Familiar landmarks were obliterated by the pall, and she could only guess which farms were burning and which had already burned. She refused to think about which would yet burn. Then she saw three figures stumbling up the path to the porch. "Thank God they're safe at least," Carrie said with relief as she went to meet them at the door.

But it wasn't Sam. It was Anna with Eric and Tim. Each of them carried a bulging gunny sack; each face was blackened and streaked with perspiration; each foot stumbled up the low steps. The boys dropped their sacks and slumped on the porch. Anna reached out to Carrie, who gathered her in her arms. She felt Anna's tears against her cheek.

They were exhausted, and no one spoke for several minutes. Then, as Anna's sobs subsided, Carrie drew her into the house and led her to one of the rockers. "I'll pour you a glass of buttermilk, Anna. It's nice and fresh. I just churned it last night."

"Thank you, Carrie," Anna murmured, as Carrie handed her the cup.

As Carrie poured buttermilk for Eric and Tim, she asked, "Anna, you've lost your house, haven't you?"

Anna pointed at the sacks by the door. "That, and a few things we loaded in the buckboard, is all we have."

"But you walked here."

120

"They needed the wagon. I left it with the men. Mr. Spreckles is letting some of his hands haul water from the wells on his ranch."

"Is Pa all right?" Carrie asked her. "Have you seen him or Will?"

"They were at my place, Carrie. They tried. They tried so hard. They beat at the flames with their own shirts, but the fire came so fast. It jumped the firebreaks as fast as they could cut them. The wind blew brands onto the roof."

A wide-eyed Eric sat at his mother's feet. "We were in the house. Mr. McLean was helping me pack my things, and a piece of the ceiling fell in, all burning. He made me leave my baseball mitt behind, the good one my papa gave me."

"I was terrified, Carrie." Anna shuddered. "I was getting the horses out of the barn, because Sam had told me we had to leave. The wind carried that big oak limb like it was a cornstalk. It landed on the house and fell through the roof right over Eric's bedroom."

"Mama was crying when we came out," Eric said. "I don't know why she was afraid. Mr. McLean was with me."

"Thank God," Anna breathed. "Oh, Carrie, if Sam hadn't been there . . ."

Carrie smoothed Anna's hair with her hands, surprised to see wisps of silver entwined in Anna's golden braids. She'd always thought of Anna as too young for her father, but now she seemed even younger and more vulnerable than Carrie herself. "Anna, it isn't fair. You've had so much trouble."

"We were making it, Carrie. We were holding on to the farm, despite the drought. Our landlord is a good man and took little rent this year, because of the small harvest. We were holding on, Carrie, and I knew in my heart that Sam was just waiting for better times."

"I know he was, Anna. He loves you, but he wanted to offer you more than debts and hard times."

"And I love him. Your papa is a proud man, though. He simply could not ask for my hand knowing I had more money than he. I do, you know."

Carrie's face must have shown her surprise. She could hardly believe that anyone with money in the bank would persist in trying to farm that God-forsaken place.

"Oh, yes, even now, with no roof over my head, I do have a little cash in the bank. Harold and I were saving to buy the farm, and there was a little insurance policy." She sighed and toyed with Eric's cowlick. "I guess we'll have to go back to Denmark now, to my family."

Anna said the same thing to Sam two days later. The fire had been stopped at the river, with the help of Mr. Spreckles' water and a long overdue bank of fog. Sam and Will slept around the clock when they returned, and now, washed and rested, they devoured the bread Anna had baked.

"It isn't that much, Sam, but it is enough for passage home for Eric and me. I don't know what else to do."

Carrie was sure her father had another suggestion. "Come on, Will, Timmie. Let's go see if we can find some eggs before dark, so we'll have them for breakfast."

"There's lots of time before dark, Carrie," Tim protested. "Besides, you don't need our help. There's only a couple of places to look."

"Come on, kids," she repeated.

Will gave his sister a knowing wink and playfully dragged Tim and Eric out the door. "Pa wants to talk to Mrs. Arnesen, dummies."

Carrie let the boys talk her into a game of hide-and-seek in the welcome cool of the evening fog. Eric had just found her in the toolshed when they heard Sam's happy shout.

"Come on back in, everybody, and help us celebrate."

It didn't take a second call. Even Tim and Eric had figured out by now why Carrie had torn them away from the supper table. They dashed to the porch where Sam stood, his arm about Anna's waist. "Guess what, everybody?"

Tears of joy sprang to Carrie's eyes.

"Mrs. Arnesen isn't going back to Denmark, is she, Pa?" Timmy asked innocently.

"No, Tim. Mrs. Arnesen and Eric are going to stay here—right here. What do you think, Will, Tim, about Mrs. Arnesen moving in here and being your new mother?"

If he'd had any doubts, their shouts settled the question. "Wow, that's great! Hey, Eric, we'll be brothers, honest-to-goodness brothers."

"It's just fine with me, Pa." Will forgot that he'd been playing hide-and-seek like a little boy a few minutes before and shook his father's hand manfully. "I'm really glad for you, for all of us."

Since Anna was living with them anyhow and times were too hard to consider an elaborate ceremony or trousseau, the wedding would be very simple. "We thought two weeks from Saturday, at the Salvation Army meeting hall. Captain Burgess will marry us," Sam explained.

"And," Anna turned to Carrie, her face glowing. "Carrie, you must stand up with me."

Soon it was the morning of Sam and Anna's wedding day. A curtain hung across the niche behind the stove where Carrie's bed stood, a bed she'd shared with Anna the past few weeks. Now she peeped around the curtain at Sam and the boys. "Don't get your best clothes dirty before you get to the church," she teased. "Now, shoo, so we can get ready."

"Where's my ma?" Eric asked.

"Hiding in there, Eric." Carrie pointed at the curtain. "It's bad luck for the groom to see his bride before the wedding."

"Can't I see her? I'm not a groom."

"Pa, get out of here so Eric can have a word with your bride." Carrie laughed as Sam playfully covered his eyes.

"I'm going on to the meeting hall then," Sam told them. "Eric can catch up with us down the road. But don't you let her be late."

Anna gave Eric a quick hug, assured him she had enough love for him and two more boys, and pushed him out after Sam, Will, and Tim. "Now, Carrie, we can be girls together one last time."

"Yes, one last time."

"Hey, not so sober. I only meant a last time as girls. In a few more hours I'll be your wicked stepmother." She turned so Carrie could help her lace her stiff corset. "But we can be friends in spite of that, Carrie."

"I know, Anna. We shall always be friends, but there is something I've been thinking about ever since you and Papa decided to get married. Well, even before that, I guess, but . . ."

"Carrie, if something about this marriage is troubling you, tell me."

"Anna, I've been thinking about leaving here. I couldn't before, because Papa and the boys needed me. But now you'll be here, and you know what they say about two women in one house."

"That's nonsense. We have been good friends for two years. We were friends before I'd even met your father, before Harold . . ."

"It isn't you, Anna. I am delighted that you are marrying my father, but any woman he might have married should be the woman of his household."

"Please, don't talk about leaving. I will not drive you out of your own home, ever."

"You're not listening, Anna. You aren't driving me out. You are giving me the opportunity to get out. I want to go back to the city."

"Carrie, I think we'd better talk about this later, with your father."

"My mind is made up. I think Papa suspects as much, but I wanted to tell you now. I wanted you to know, before you promise yourself to Papa, that this will be your house. Of course, I will be your friend, but I will not be here, in your way. I wanted to tell you because, in your place, I think I would want that."

"Carrie," Anna protested.

"And you want it too. Now don't think you have to lie about it in order to be nice. Of course, you want some privacy. You want to do things your own way in your own house."

Anna blushed, and looked at the little sleeping niche.

"Yes, Anna, I thought about that too. You'll only have a couple of days over in Monterey, and then where did you plan to sleep? In the bedroom with three little boys?"

"Well, no."

"Well, I'm not going to!" Carrie laughed. "So, now that's settled. Let's get you dressed."

Anna faced the small oval mirror as Carrie brushed her hair into an unaccustomed pompadour. "Carrie, have you told Matt?"

"Told Matt what?" Carrie said, a little too brusquely.

"That you are leaving Soledad."

"Not yet." It was going to be hard to leave Matt behind, but then, he hadn't given her a sign in months that he cared. "I suppose I'll tell him today, after the wedding."

"He isn't going to like it."

"I doubt he'll care much."

"He'll care a great deal, Carrie. He loves you."

"Oh, he does?" Carrie snapped. "He hasn't told me about it." Carrie remembered New Year's Eve, but that had been so long ago. "We hardly see him anymore."

"He's working very hard. He goes anywhere from Castroville to King City, working with the drillers."

"That's what Matt Hanlon's in love with, Anna." *Last spring he was still talking about "our" farm*, she recalled, and her eyes watered. *But that was last spring.* "Wells!" she continued flatly. "That's all he's talked about as long as I've known him. Wells, and his crazy dream that this desolation is just waiting for him to turn it into paradise."

"While you talk to him about reality, Carrie," Anna reminded her. "You always put down his dreams, so he's determined to give you what you want—reality. Don't throw away Matt's love. That kind seldom comes once in a lifetime, for all I have been blessed with it twice."

"I can't throw away what I don't have. What you think you see between Matt and me is as unreal as that farm of his." Carrie put the final hairpin into Anna's hair. "Now, let's be off to your wedding."

Chapter Thirteen

*C*aptain Lucy Burgess played "The Wedding March" on her accordion. Carrie walked down the aisle of the Army meeting hall toward the captain. Anna followed on Eric's arm. Carrie smiled at her father, who was shifting from foot to foot as he waited for his bride.

Matt stood next to him, turned out in a navy blue serge suit and high starched collar that must have been borrowed. Carrie realized she had never seen Matt dressed up before. He did look fine, erect and proud, his red hair glowing in the candlelight.

For just a second Carrie imagined him standing there waiting for her. She wanted to search his face, to see if he, too, was thinking of their own wedding, but his eyes were cast downward as if to avoid her look.

As Captain Burgess performed the brief marriage ceremony, Carrie tried to ignore Matt's closeness. Instead, she concentrated on her own plans for the future, plans that must exclude him.

It seemed right that Sam and Anna should pool their meager resources and rebuild their lives together. *But,* Carrie promised herself, *I will have more. I'll work hard now to better myself. I'll support myself and show them all that I can make a good life for myself.*

She looked at Matt again, but he still avoided her glance. *Besides,* she thought, *Matt's forgotten all about New Year's Eve. He's said nothing in months about us.*

When Carrie had finished serving the slices of rich fruitcake and cups of steaming tea to the handful of wedding guests, she reluctantly sought out Matt. As usual, he held an audience of boys and young men with his tales of the prosperity that was "just around the corner."

"Mr. Hanlon, when you've a few minutes I'd like to speak with you."

He seemed mildly annoyed by the interruption. "Sure, Miss Carrie. Some mischief for the honeymooners?" he teased half-heartedly, as he followed her outside.

"No, nothing like that. I just wanted to tell you something." He still refused to look at her, and she found herself longing to see, again, that penetrating, knowing stare. "Matt, I'm leaving Fort Romie."

She thought she heard the gasp, though he stifled it immediately. He finally looked at her, and she told herself there was panic, for just an instant, in those cold eyes. "Leaving Fort Romie! Carrie, you can't mean that. Why?"

"Isn't it obvious? I've only stayed this long because Papa and the boys needed me. Now Anna will be the woman in my father's house. So I am free to go back to the city."

"But you can't leave, Carrie!" She saw that his fists were clenched, and he bit his lower lip as if to hold back his words. Finally, with a determined calm, he spoke. "What will you do there?" he asked. "It was a hard life before, working in the shop and living with your family, but alone? San Francisco is no place for a young woman alone."

"Don't be silly, Mr. Hanlon." Carrie blurted out the flippant answer. *Why doesn't he talk about his dream now?* she wondered. He could have stopped her with a word—a teasing, jesting, too-personal word. But instead he was making it easy for her to hide her own pain behind a glib toss of her head. "There are any number of respectable boardinghouses, and they aren't all that expensive," she assured him. "I expect no difficulty finding a job, since the Emporium was quite satisfied with my work before."

"But it's such hard work, Carrie, shut up indoors for ten or twelve hours a day, on your feet all the time. You can't go back to that."

"Thank you for your concern," she mocked. "But thousands of girls do it all the time."

"And waste away with consumption too. Carrie," he pleaded, "please don't do that to yourself."

"I really can't stay on anyhow." *It's nice of him to worry about me, at least,* she reflected. *Once I thought he would gladly take me straight to the poorhouse with him, but now he's quite the sensible gentleman.* "You know what they say about two women in one house," she continued.

"They don't mean you and Anna. You're good friends. She'll never drive you out of your father's home."

131

"No, she never would, but I know they need their privacy now. There just isn't room. And besides, I have plans. I'm going to save so I can go to a school and learn typewriting. Then I can get a good job in an office. The hours are shorter and the pay is better." Somehow it didn't sound as good to her as it had when Matt wasn't around. "I'll be just fine."

"Carrie." His hands reached for hers and then dropped. He looked at them, not at her, as he spoke again. "Then all I can do is wish you the best of luck. All I want is for you to be happy."

Again, he could have stopped her with that fumbled touch. She still hoped he would. But instead he sighed and shuffled back indoors.

"Well, so much for Matt Hanlon's loving me." Carrie whispered, blinking away her tears. Then she squared her shoulders and headed home to begin packing.

She spent the next three days scrubbing the cabin from top to bottom. The first fall rain began on Sunday evening, and she knew Sam and Anna, at the hotel over in Monterey, would think it more beautiful than the bluest sky.

They were to return on the Tuesday train. Will was proud to be trusted to drive Anna's smart team to town that morning. He would meet the train and drive them home after school. Carrie dreaded telling her father that night that she had already bought her train ticket to San Francisco.

"I've been loafing for days, Carrie. Now it's my turn to do the dishes," Anna insisted, as Carrie began to clear the supper table. "Sit a while and talk to your papa." Anna smiled and nodded to Carrie.

"Papa." She began the speech she'd been rehearsing for three days. "Papa, you know how I've been talking about going back to the city and getting a job there."

"Foolish talk, Carrie. You're not going back there and work in a shop again."

"Papa, I really want to go, and now that you and the boys don't need me here . . ."

"I may have taken another wife, but that doesn't mean you are not wanted here," Sam insisted.

"I didn't say 'wanted,' Papa. I said I am not needed here, and that's true. Anyhow," Carrie threw a glance toward her stove corner bedstead. "Anyhow, there isn't that much room."

Sam smiled at her reference. "We'll manage that, never fear. Anna and I are in full agreement, Carrie, that we will make room for all our family."

"Papa, I want to go. And I already have my ticket bought and my trunk packed. I'm leaving tomorrow."

Anna came back to the table now, hands folded under her apron, and Carrie turned to her. "Anna, you understand. Tell him it's best."

"What did you know about this, Anna?" Sam asked.

"Now, Sam, you know I'd love to have Carrie stay on with us. But she told me before the wedding that she wanted to go back to the city. And perhaps it isn't such a bad idea."

"To go back to work selling ladies' gloves ten hours a day?" Sam demanded. "Anna, what are you thinking?"

"Carrie, do you still want to learn typewriting?" Anna fumbled with something under her apron.

"Why, yes, Anna, eventually, after I've saved some money for school."

"Well, Carrie, I've done a little thinking too. I've offered Harold's insurance money to Sam to put into the farm, but he won't take it. He says I should invest it, for Eric. So I'd like to invest it in you."

"What do you mean by that?"

"I mean I'd like to lend you enough so you can go to school right away." She handed Carrie an embroidered coin purse. Carrie could feel several hard, round coins, which she presumed were five dollar gold pieces. "Then, when you're settled into a good job, you can pay me back, with interest. When Eric is old enough to set out on his own, it will be there for him. Meantime, you'll be that much ahead with your own plans."

Carrie hesitated. After all, Sam had refused to use Anna's legacy. Now his fingers drummed the table as he looked from the rain-dampened fields to the bedstead in the corner. Then he looked fondly at his bride. "Anna, that money should be Eric's."

"And so it will be," Anna promised. "But it's better Carrie should use it now than that it be hidden away in a mattress."

"And, Carrie, are you sure this is what you want to do?" her father asked.

"Absolutely." She denied the prickle of doubt even to herself. "I miss the excitement of the city, Papa. I want nice clothes and bright lights around me and music and happy people." *Well, I do*, she told herself. *Maybe I'd rather have them with Matt, but . . .* "And I will pay Anna back every cent. I promise you that."

"What about Matt? I'd always hoped you two would . . ."

Why did he have to ask that? Carrie avoided her father's eyes. "I told him the day you were married that I was going. He just wished me luck."

Sam was glum, his lips taut. He studied first his daughter's face, then his wife's. Turning back to Carrie, he spoke. "All right, Carrie. I guess I'm outvoted. But never forget, daughter, if it doesn't work out, you've always a home in my house."

As the train chugged heavily up the grade out of the Salinas Valley, Carrie looked back at the narrow rift, hills climbing sharply both east and west, the trail of dark green willow trees marking the path of the twisting river. *Capricious river, appearing and disappearing at the whim of the Almighty,* she huffed.

More than two years ago she had come south on this train, thinking the bright sun a good omen. Now she knew the leaden skies and steady drip, drip of the rain promised infinitely more, at least to the loved ones she left behind.

She clutched Anna's little hoard of gold pieces. It would be enough, carefully husbanded, to pay a few weeks' board and room and tuition at one of the new business schools along Market Street.

Chapter Fourteen

*C*arrie tried not to stare at the straining elevator cables sliding slowly behind the iron grillwork. With a screech that set her teeth on edge, the cage reversed direction for an instant and jolted to a stop.

"Street floor, miss." The elevator operator tugged the polished brass lever that opened the door and tipped his hat. "Watch your step now."

Carrie crossed the gleaming black and white tiled foyer floor. It would have been nice to go to work every day in the Crocker Building, one of San Francisco's new skyscrapers, but she wouldn't let herself be discouraged. This was only her first job interview, so it did not matter that the answer was that the position was already filled.

She wrapped the rabbit-fur trimmed cloak her old friend Betsy had lent her tightly against a sharp February wind off the bay and skipped the scattered puddles left from yesterday's rain. The sky was now a brilliant cerulean blue spattered with wisps of cotton clouds. These crisp, crystal clear days between the winter rains were her favorite San Francisco weather; she carried her typist's certificate and a letter of recommendation from the school; and her next appointment was with a Mr. Hempstead. She consulted the slip of paper with the address on it again. "Pier Four," she read.

Carrie was heady with the salty sea smell. Horsecars clanged as they passed, headed down Market Street, just as she was, for the busy docks. She hurried across California Street as a rowdy bell dinged impatiently, heralding the approach of a cable car. If she got this job, she thought, maybe she could afford to take the cable car back up to Mrs. Hurley's.

"I'm living at Mrs. Hurley's boardinghouse, just off California Street," Carrie told Mr. Hempstead, in answer to his question.

"Oh, yes, I know the place. A fine lady, known for running a thoroughly respectable boardinghouse. But isn't it a bit expensive?" the dignified gray-haired man behind the broad oak desk inquired.

"I am sharing a room with an old friend, a girl I used to work with at the Emporium. That makes the cost less."

"I see. You have no family here in the city, then?"

"No, sir. My father has a farm near Soledad, in the Salinas Valley."

Mr. Hempstead glanced at her application again. "That wouldn't be the Sam McLean I knew several years ago, a teamster?"

"My father used to be a teamster here, but he resettled about three years ago."

"Married one of the Bennett girls?"

"Why, yes, Mr. Hempstead. Elizabeth Bennett was my mother. She died some time ago."

"Yes, I heard that. And Sam had a run of bad luck, too, as I recall. But he was always talking about having a farm one day. So he made it." Mr. Hempstead smiled reassuringly at Carrie. "I'm glad to hear that."

He scanned the letter again. "Country life too tame for you, Miss McLean?"

"Not exactly, sir. But I was raised here. And my father remarried recently."

He nodded knowingly, and Carrie knew what he was thinking. She resisted the temptation to defend Anna. It was, after all, none of his business why she chose to support herself in San Francisco rather than staying with Papa.

"Well, Miss McLean, your instructor speaks highly of your abilities, and I knew your Grandfather Bennett well. So, if you like, we'll be happy to try you in the position. Your duties will be to typewrite all of our business correspondence, bills to our customers, checks for my signature. You will also answer the telephone and receive customers and salesmen, so your appearance must always be neat and decorous, and your behavior above reproach."

He gave her an almost fatherly smile. "But I can tell from this brief meeting that you know how to present yourself. You are truly your mother's daughter. Now, let me show you around Hempstead and Sloane."

As they went through the outer office, a pretty young woman sat at the typewriter. Carrie assumed she was the one who was leaving to be married. At a second desk, a

139

young man hunched over a massive ledger, painstakingly entering numbers.

Outside, a three-masted schooner stood proudly at anchor. Steamships were taking over the bay, Carrie knew, but sails were still seen now and then. Her eyes followed the tall masts, their booms wrapped with furled sail, up into the blue sky.

"She's a beauty, isn't she?" Mr. Hempstead said. "One of the last of her kind, I fear. Her captain doesn't like the sound or smell of the steamers and, for now, there's not that much hurry getting the lumber down the coast. Soon they'll all be gone, though, those graceful ladies of the waves."

Carrie took care not to get Betsy's cloak soiled as they walked among tall stacks of pungent redwood planks. Hempstead and Sloane, she learned, owned a sawmill up on the Mendocino Coast, where they cut the great redwood trees from which most of San Francisco was built. The rough lumber was shipped south in a fleet of schooners and barges that shuttled back and forth constantly. They docked here to unload the valuable cargo and load supplies for the mill and the lumber camps.

Carrie watched, agape, as laborers in red plaid flannel shirts steadied the huge bundles of rust-colored boards being hoisted from a ship's hold by winch. "Stay back, Miss McLean," Mr. Hempstead warned. "Unloading lumber is dangerous work."

She really didn't need to be told that one slip of the rope that bound the planks could send several hundred pounds of wood down on the dock like a set of jackstraws. Yet the men seldom spoke. Each one seemed to know

140

exactly where he belonged and what he must do to set the cargo down safely.

A well-dressed man wandered among the stacks, scribbling on a small yellow pad. "A customer?" Carrie asked.

"We sell wholesale exclusively, Miss McLean," her new boss explained. "That man owns a lumberyard out in the Mission district. He buys most of his stock from us. We also sell directly to contractors, who come here to inspect our stock and place their orders. We employ the dock workers and teamsters who do our deliveries, as well as the ships' crews and the mill workers in Mendocino."

He helped Carrie over a coil of rope and started back to the office. "So you will be meeting a lot of people. But please don't do what our last typewriter operator did, and get yourself engaged right away." He smiled and winked. "We don't want to lose you too quickly."

They stepped back inside. "We will see you next Monday morning, then. Miss Stevens will be here for one week more to show you the work."

The pretty girl looked up from her typewriter and smiled as Mr. Hempstead continued. "Miss Stevens, this is Miss McLean, your replacement."

The man who sat at the other desk lifted his head, then. "And, Miss McLean, this is our bookkeeper, Roger Morgan."

Mr. Morgan stood and bowed slightly. "I am very pleased to meet you, Miss McLean." His serious hazel eyes dropped as he smiled somewhat shyly.

Perhaps it was Mr. Hempstead's teasing about meeting "lots of people," but Carrie found herself studying Mr.

Morgan as he sat down and picked up his pen. He was rather tall with a fair complexion. *Probably from working indoors so much,* she thought. He had almost delicate blond lashes and a small, golden mustache. His sandy brown hair was slicked flat from the sharp, straight center part. There was just a hint of a cleft in the firm chin that was held high by his stiffly starched collar. So different from Matt.

Well, she asked herself, *is that bad?* Celluloid sleeves protected his snow-white cuffs which peeked from under his impeccably pressed suit jacket. Either he had a fantastic laundry or he was already married, Carrie thought, as she shook hands with Mr. Hempstead. "I'll be here at 8:00 on Monday, sir. And thank you."

Chapter Fifteen

*C*arrie was glad she had saved that one good suit through the hard years in Soledad. The deep green velveteen was becoming to her, she knew. Mr. Morgan had been most flattering when he called for her at Mrs. Hurley's after supper, and he would feel no shame in comparing her appearance to that of the other young ladies at the lecture.

Carrie carefully kept her eyes forward, watching the views projected on the wall behind the speaker. But she did get glimpses, off to the side, of Roger glancing her way now and then.

The last picture disappeared, and the lights came on in the hall, as the speaker finished his description of the glories of the great Rocky Mountains. "Most interesting, don't you think, Miss McLean?"

"Oh, yes, Mr. Morgan. Such magnificent peaks and lovely lakes. And I should certainly like to see those spouts of steam for myself."

"Strange phenomena, indeed." He offered his arm as they left the auditorium. "But a long journey. I am content to stay here in San Francisco and let others do the exploring."

"Have you never traveled at all, Mr. Morgan?"

"I've been up into the woods, to the sawmill in Mendocino a few times, on business. And to Sacramento."

"I've never been anywhere, except through San Jose and Salinas City going to Soledad and back."

"That must be very different from San Francisco. Is it mostly farms?" he inquired politely.

"There are little farms and orchards along the way as far as San Jose, and some pleasant towns. After that, it's pretty much bare hills and that wind-swept valley, alternately sun-blasted and fog-smothered. That isn't traveling but . . ."

Carrie recalled Matt's tales, more fascinating than the speaker's lecture. "I used to know someone who had been all over the country—New York, Chicago. He gave my brothers a set of stereopticon pictures of the Yosemite Valley once."

"A gentleman friend?"

"A family friend," she said a little too quickly, "my father's friend, really." Carrie felt her heart jump at the white lie, but Mr. Morgan didn't seem to notice her agitation.

"I, ah, I see." He really was a shy man. Carrie had been with Hempstead and Sloane for nearly three months, and this was the first time he'd asked her out, though he'd obviously been watching her, with some approval, since their first meeting. "I was afraid you had, perhaps, an understanding with someone, and I wouldn't presume to force my attentions."

"Nonsense, Mr. Morgan. I'm totally unattached," she assured him. "And I have enjoyed this evening and your company very much."

He didn't suggest taking a cable car, but it was a balmy late spring evening anyhow. Carrie still found the once familiar salt breeze exciting, and here and there down the cross streets she could see the moon reflected on the rippling bay. As they detoured around the steep-walled valley between the theater and her boardinghouse, Carrie wondered if the rumors she heard of what went on behind the walls of the rough Chinatown tenements were really true. She held Roger Morgan's arm just a little more tightly as they skirted the edge of the congested settlement.

"I'm sorry, Miss McLean. You're tired. We should have taken a car, but it seemed such a pleasant evening."

"Oh, I'm not tired at all," she told him. "It is a beautiful night, and we're nearly there already."

"It's that one on the corner, isn't it?" he asked.

"Yes, right here." He walked her to the front steps. "Thank you for your invitation, Mr. Morgan."

"I hope to have the pleasure of your company again soon, Miss McLean."

"I'd like that. Thank you again."

"Well," Betsy demanded the minute Carrie closed the door to their room. "How did it go?"

"How did what go?" Carrie countered casually.

"Your evening out with the bookkeeper, silly. Did he like you? Did he ask you out again? Are you going?"

"I guess he likes me well enough." Carrie shrugged. "He did ask me to the lecture after all. And he didn't specifically ask me out again, but he did hint that he would."

"Just hinted?" Betsy prodded.

"He said he hoped to have the pleasure of my company again soon. Is that good enough for you, Bets?"

"Mmmm. Promising." Betsy winked. "He does sound exciting."

Carrie had to laugh.

"What's so funny, Carrie?"

"'Exciting' isn't exactly the word I'd use to describe Roger Morgan."

"But he's nice, isn't he? And he's got a good job, and he just might be thinking about courting you."

"All that might be exciting, I guess, if true," Carrie agreed. "But Mr. Morgan himself! No, 'exciting' just doesn't suit him."

"What do you mean by that? You said he was nice."

"Very nice, Betsy. He's a perfect gentleman, with good prospects. But I'd hardly call one travelogue a court-ship."

"So it may take a little time." Betsy shrugged. "I'm still working on the bachelor in the upstairs front, and he moved in before Christmas."

"All right. I admit it. By those standards Mr. Morgan is a fast worker." Carrie chuckled again, but her mind was not on Roger.

"Come back, Carrie. You look like you're a million miles away."

"I guess I was," Carrie admitted.

"Making wedding plans?"

"Hardly."

"But you do like him, don't you?" Betsy giggled.

"Sure, I like him, Betsy. I said he was a perfect gentleman."

"Such enthusiasm!" Betsy's voice was more serious now. "Carrie, what about that man you wrote me about from Soledad?"

"I guess we've been friends so long you can read my mind, Betsy. I was thinking about Matt. They are so different. The first time I saw Matt he teased me. And after that he kept making excuses to call, or at least I thought they were excuses."

"Then why didn't you marry him?"

"He never asked me."

"You wrote a year ago Christmastime that he gave you a watch and told you he loved you."

"Yes, he did." Carrie bit her lip as she recalled the passion of Matt's kisses that New Year's Eve. "But then he lost his job, and times were so bad."

"I always thought true love was supposed to conquer hard times."

"So did I. And Matt certainly claimed so, always insisting he was going to buy a farm for us and talking about a honeymoon."

"So how can you say he never asked you to marry him?"

"He didn't. He talked about it in a roundabout way, but he never asked me. I thought maybe, when I told him I was moving back here, he'd try to stop me. But he just wished me luck."

"You love him, don't you, Carrie?"

"Maybe." *Maybe that's why I keep thinking of him whenever I look at Roger,* Carrie thought, as she warmed at the memory of Matt's touch. "I guess I thought I did," she sighed. "But, Betsy, Matt's no good, not for me anyhow."

"Roger is?"

"Roger is his exact opposite. Matt's got blue eyes, cold blue with a glint of ice; Roger's are soft hazel. Matt's hair is carrot red and never looks combed, and Roger never has a lock out of place. Matt is always dreaming or scheming. He's so sure of himself, so sure God is his personal friend and has all these great things in store for him. But Roger works. He's steady and reliable. Matt insists he'll have a farm someday, but Roger already has a house, or at least his mother does."

"Oh? His mother?"

"So he lives with his mother. What's wrong with a man being good to his mother?" Carrie defended.

"Nothing. Nothing at all, as long as he isn't too good to her."

"Matt never even knew his mother," Carrie mused. "He was raised in an orphanage."

"Carrie, are you sure you shouldn't go back to Fort Romie? At least see him again before you do anything foolish."

"No!" Carrie hadn't meant to snap at her. "Any romantic notions I ever had about Matt Hanlon are over and done with. I think he was relieved to see me leave. And letting Roger Morgan court me, if he does, could hardly be considered foolish. Why, he's one of the firm's most trusted employees. What with Mr. Hempstead getting up in years and having no children, I shouldn't be surprised if Roger Morgan were manager, or maybe even a partner one day."

Now Betsy was grinning. "Listen to yourself, Carrie. Just who is doing the dreaming now?"

Carrie brushed Betsy's question out of her mind several times over the next weeks, just as she brushed Matt Hanlon's teasing grin and penetrating stare from her memories. Roger did ask her out again, and again.

It was a cool, foggy Sunday morning, typical of San Francisco in July. Carrie dressed nervously, brushing and rebrushing the brown serge skirt lest any trace of lint cling to it. She settled her new bonnet behind her pompadour, shifted its angle, and pinned it firmly. She was going to church with Roger and his mother before joining them for Sunday dinner. Roger cared a great deal for his mother, Carrie knew. Now he was taking Carrie to meet her.

Carrie had gotten lazy about going to church since Sunday was the only day she could sleep late. In fact, she hadn't been to the big stone church the Morgans attended since her mother had taken her there as a little girl. She thought of her mother as she and Roger walked up the broad steps. She wished Liz could be here now to meet Roger and his mother. Carrie thought her mother would have approved.

The Morgan house was a sturdy, two-story clapboard on Dolores Street, near the old mission. As the three of them sat around the heavy oak table in the dining room after the service, Carrie admired the fine blue and white china. "My mother had a set just like it," she explained, not adding that she had sold the precious china the year before to keep food on the McLeans' pine table.

"It was very fashionable about the time I was married, and I still love it dearly," Mrs. Morgan purred. "But then, as you can see, I like to keep my old things around me. I came to this house as a bride, and I don't think I could bear to leave it."

"I don't blame you, Mrs. Morgan. It's charming."

Carrie looked around at the lace tablecloth, lace curtains at the bay window, and the piano in the parlor. She knew it didn't compare with the new mansions lining Van Ness. It was just an ordinary tradesman's house, but compared to the cabin at Fort Romie, not to mention the south of Market Street flat that Carrie had grown up in, it was luxurious.

"Do you play, Carrie?" Mrs. Morgan asked, nodding toward the piano. "I can't anymore because of my rheumatism."

"No, Mrs. Morgan. I'm afraid I never learned. It's a lovely instrument."

"Yes. My dear husband always insisted on the best, and so does dear Roger. It's too bad you don't play. It needs use."

"You keep everything so nice, Mrs. Morgan," Carrie said. "It must be hard work, with such a large house."

150

"Thank you, Carrie dear, but I could never do it by myself. Roger simply insists that we have a day girl in for cleaning and the laundry. He's such a devoted son."

"Now, Mama, it's no more than you deserve." Roger seemed embarrassed. "Miss Carrie, would you like to see the garden?"

Chapter Sixteen

A few evenings later Betsy and Carrie were sewing in the back bedroom they shared at Mrs. Hurley's boarding-house. "You must have made a good impression on Mrs. Morgan," Betsy observed.

"Oh, Betsy, don't be silly. I just spent Sunday afternoon with Roger and his mother. That's all."

"That's all." Betsy giggled as she stuck another pin in the hem of Carrie's new gown. "And now you have to have this dress done before Saturday evening because Roger is taking you to see John Drew at the Orpheum."

"Wouldn't you want a new dress if you were going to see John Drew?"

"Why? You're going to see him. He isn't going to see you." Betsy stuffed more pins in her mouth and concentrated on the five-yard sweep of Carrie's skirt.

"I think she liked me, Bets. Of course she's too much of a lady to let on if she didn't, but somehow I don't think Roger would keep seeing me if she disapproved."

Betsy grunted and shook her head.

"A man who is thoughtful of his mother would be thoughtful of his wife too." Carrie turned in front of the mirror as Betsy pinned. "Do you think this neckline is all right? It's a little lower than I'm used to."

"Quit worrying about that décolletage. It's not as low as most of my customers'. Besides, it's for Roger, not his mama. Do you, or do you not, want him to propose after the play?"

"He did say the theater and supper," Carrie mused. "Usually he doesn't want to be out that late. That could mean he has something in mind."

"And being a perfect gentleman, what else could he have in mind but a proposal?" Betsy winked as she stuck the last pin in the pale green silk. "Oooh, I do like this dress. You know, you could use that same pattern for a wedding dress. Just put a lace insert at the neckline, and lengthen the pleat over the bustle into a train."

Carrie stifled a sigh, remembering that she'd spent the five dollars that should have gone to Anna that month on the silk for this dress. "I really shouldn't spend so much on clothes when I'm still in debt to my stepmother, Betsy. She was so good to lend me her nest egg."

"Once you're married to Roger he can pay that all back easily."

"He doesn't know anything about it, Betsy. I just can't tell him how poor we've been. No, I can't marry him until I've repaid her."

"Well, I wouldn't feel guilty. You've had about three new dresses since you started working for Hempstead and

Sloane. And your family's doing well enough this year to pay for your wedding dress anyhow."

"They do seem to be doing well at last, thank God. But there is one hundred dollars due on the farm next month, and that's a lot of money even with a good harvest."

"A Christmas wedding would be nice," Betsy suggested.

"I've been thinking about that, Betsy. But it would be hard to have the debt paid by then. No, I think I will stall him a while."

"Ever the eager bride."

"No need to be sarcastic. Why should I be in a big hurry?"

"Maybe so he won't change his mind."

"Not too likely." Carrie shrugged. "Roger's a decent catch, but he isn't the only man in the world."

"So maybe you're afraid you'll change your mind."

Betsy had come uncomfortably close to the truth. There was at least one other man in the world. *No, there isn't*, she told herself. Matt didn't care about her anymore. He hadn't even written to her since she'd left Soledad, not even after she'd written her father and Anna that she was seeing Roger.

"I only mean to put Roger off for a demure few weeks while I make certain of my modest feelings," she assured Betsy. "Then I'll tell him I will marry him, but I always wanted to be a June bride. Come June, Anna will be repaid, and I can afford a wedding."

"Would you be so patient if you were planning to marry your wild red-headed farmer?" wondered Betsy.

"What in the world has Matt got to do with it?" Carrie responded curtly, clearly impatient with Betsy's question. "Anyhow, it wouldn't be a question of my patience if I were marrying Matt. It would be his, and he never had any."

"Roger, on the other hand . . ."

"Roger is a gentleman, something no one ever accused Matt Hanlon of being."

Yes, Carrie thought, as she lay in bed that night, *Roger is everything Matt wasn't—steady, reliable, thoughtful.* But it was Matt whose caress she felt as she fell asleep.

The small restaurant was thronged with after-theater patrons, which seemed to surprise Roger. They were seated at the table nearest the kitchen door, and busy waiters rushed back and forth, frequently bumping Roger's chair, as he faced Carrie across plates of chilled poached salmon and warm biscuits.

"I'm terribly sorry, Miss Carrie. I didn't realize it would be so crowded and noisy here."

"It's all right, Mr. Morgan. I rather like the excitement." She smiled reassurance. "Wasn't the play wonderful? Mr. Drew is such a great actor."

"Yes, yes, quite thrilling." He toyed with a slice of salmon, then broke a biscuit. The butter knife slipped from his hand and dropped to the floor. Though the clink could scarcely be heard with all the other noises, he flushed. "Oh, I'm so clumsy," he apologized, as a waiter approached.

"No, thank you," he said, as the waiter offered a clean knife. "I believe we are finished anyhow. May I . . ." Then he turned to Carrie quickly. "Unless you would like an ice or something, Miss Carrie?"

"No, thank you, Mr. Morgan. I have had quite enough for so late in the evening."

He was visibly relieved. "May I have the check, then?"

Outside, much to Carrie's surprise, Roger hailed a cab. "As you said, Miss Carrie, it is quite late," he murmured, helping her in. They rode several blocks in a silence that was broken every few moments by a deep breath from Roger. Then he swallowed audibly and spoke. "Miss Carrie, I am truly sorry about the restaurant."

"But there is no reason to be. The supper was delicious and the service excellent."

"But there were so many people, so much noise. I had hoped we could have some privacy." He gulped again and fumbled in his pocket. "Miss Carrie, I wanted an opportunity to speak with you about something of the greatest importance."

"Oh, Mr. Morgan, something important?" Carrie feigned proper maidenly amazement.

"Yes. Miss Carrie, we have been keeping company for some months now, and I find you a most pleasant companion. You are an attractive woman of excellent manner and noble character."

It was a set speech like Captain Stoneham's. *Did men always memorize their proposals?* Carrie wondered. *Matt wouldn't have.*

"Miss Carrie, I have become very fond of you. I would be pleased and honored if you would consent to be my wife."

157

Why shouldn't men memorize their proposals? her rational mind continued. Demurely she murmured her rehearsed answer. "Mr. Morgan, you have literally taken my breath away. I'd no idea you thought of me in that way."

"B-b-but," he stammered. "But you and I are so suited to each other. I am certain I could make you happy, Miss Carrie. I would certainly try my best."

Carrie smiled, modestly she hoped. "Please, Mr. Morgan. Your offer is most generous, but you have taken me by surprise. Such a decision must be carefully considered. Please let me have a little time, a few days, to sort out my thoughts."

"Oh, of course, Miss Carrie. I shouldn't dream of pressing you for an answer." He fumbled in his pocket again, and she guessed he had already purchased an engagement ring. "Perhaps next Saturday afternoon we could walk in the park. Might I hope to have your answer by then?"

That week a letter came from Anna. They had made the mortgage payment out of the money from the sugar beet harvest, and the larder was well stocked for winter. But Sam did want to buy another cow, and the three boys all needed new school clothes because they were growing so fast.

The following Saturday, Carrie pleaded a headache, and went directly home when the office closed at 1:00. Roger was disappointed, but she needed a little more time. "Not to think, of course," she confided to Betsy the next afternoon, "but to delay the wedding. I simply have to pay Anna back first."

The following Saturday afternoon was warm and sunny. "A typical autumn afternoon," Carrie remarked, as Roger helped her aboard a trolley bound for Golden Gate Park. "I'm told the rest of the world has warm summer and cool spring and fall."

"So they say, Miss Carrie. But San Francisco is delightfully different. It would be hard to imagine a finer day than this one."

They had boarded the trolley on Market Street near the massive Palace Hotel, and Carrie briefly wondered if, as Roger's wife, she could someday afford to dine at its famous crystal-domed dining room.

They rode through the city's "slot," the broad swath cut between the hills by Market Street and named for the cable car slot that ran down the middle of the wide street. Carrie did love the city, and she looked around, proud of its vitality and vigor. Behind her she could see the clock tower of the Ferry Building, where passengers shuttled across San Francisco Bay.

The trolley carried them past new brick skyscrapers, some ten or twelve stories high, where the business of the city, state, and whole Pacific Coast was transacted. Then the handsomely domed Emporium. Maybe Carrie would be a frequent customer soon and never again just a humble shop girl.

Market Street ran straight toward Twin Peaks, but their route took them down Van Ness Avenue. As they turned Roger pointed to the massive dome that topped the gray limestone building so splendidly columned and decorated with gargoyles. "I think we must have the finest city hall in the whole country, don't you?"

159

Carrie nodded absently as she turned to catch glimpses of the mansions that stretched along the tree-lined avenue toward the bay. The great turreted, bay-windowed homes belonged to the bankers, railroad executives, and landowners who ruled the city. Mr. Spreckles had built a marvelous house here, she'd heard—a four-story wonder with mansard roof and pediment-crowned dormers. *Yes*, she thought, *Matt's old boss has made good money.*

"I wonder if he ever thinks of the poor people who slave all their lives on his land and in his sugar mill," she muttered.

But Roger didn't seem to have heard, and Carrie's thoughts returned to her own problems. *Not that I really have problems*, she thought. *Any woman would feel herself very fortunate to be marrying such a nice gentleman with such good prospects. Anna said there must be love in a marriage*, she recalled. *Well, she certainly liked Roger, and she could learn to love him.*

Her reverie was interrupted as the trolley reached the end of the line, out where straggling cottages gave way to the open space of Golden Gate Park, which was rapidly reclaiming the sandy wasteland.

"There is a showing of chrysanthemums at the conservatory," Roger said with little enthusiasm as he handed her down from the trolley. "Or . . ."

"Let's just walk a while," she offered. "It's really rather warm, and I would enjoy the shade."

Most of the trees had been planted within Carrie's short lifetime, but the quick-growing eucalyptus wind-breaks had already tamed the sand dunes. "Do you re-

160

member how the sand used to blow all over this part of the city when we were children? It has grown into such a beautiful place in the past few years, hasn't it?"

"Yes," he agreed somewhat impatiently. "The city is fortunate to have Mr. McLaren as park superintendent."

They had entered the glade that would blaze with rhododendron the next spring. Now it was a serene refuge, shaded with maturing live oaks. Carrie sat in an emerald alcove formed by the shrubs and pulled Roger down beside her.

"Miss Carrie," he stammered. "It has been two weeks now."

"I know, Mr. Morgan. I should not have kept you waiting so long, but I wanted to be very sure." He fixed his eyes on her hands. "Yes, Mr. Morgan, I will be honored to be your wife."

She did expect a kiss, at least, but he only lifted her hand and brushed it with trembling lips. "Thank you, Miss Carrie. You have made me very happy, and I assure you you will never regret your decision. I took the liberty, Miss Carrie, of anticipating your answer."

He reached into his waistcoat pocket and pulled out a jeweler's box. "I do hope it is the right size." He opened the box and handed her a small leather case. Carrie recalled a delicate bowknot watch still hidden in her trunk but quickly brushed the thought aside as she opened the case.

"Roger! How beautiful!" Carrie looked at the gold band set with a large, brilliant diamond. How could she doubt her decision? "But isn't it rather extravagant?"

"Nothing is too good for my wife, Carrie." His voice quivered as he spoke, and Carrie wasn't imagining the moisture in his eyes.

"Will you put it on for me, Roger?"

Roger did not protest her suggestion of a June wedding. "Of course I understand, dearest. A woman needs time to prepare for her wedding day."

Not eight months, Carrie thought. "You are so good to me, Roger, and so patient. But the time will pass quickly, and then we shall be so happy together."

They agreed not to announce their engagement at the office until later. "No need to complicate our working together," Roger explained. "It would be better, I think, if they did not know until spring. Then you will want to stop working anyway, to get ready for the wedding."

Roger continued to treat Carrie with distant courtesy at the office, but away from work he became surprisingly tender. And he was generous, too, insisting on her accepting expensive gifts.

"I know what it cost, Betsy," Carrie defended, as she showed her friend the shimmery soft fox fur wrap he'd given her for Christmas. "But he insists he can afford it. Oh, Betsy, it's as if all my dreams were coming true all at once."

"That is a beautiful cape, Miss McLean," Mr. Hempstead commented on a Saturday afternoon early in the New Year. "A Christmas gift?"

"Why, yes, Mr. Hempstead. A Christmas gift." He seemed to be waiting for more of an explanation. What was he thinking anyhow? "From my family. The harvest was very good last fall."

"I see." He nodded. "Miss McLean, could I speak with you in my office for a moment before you leave?"

Carrie followed him through the inner door. "Mr. Hempstead," she stammered, "is anything wrong, about my work or anything?"

"Your work has been excellent, Miss McLean. But I do have a question." He took a small stack of papers from a desk drawer. "Miss McLean, have you ever seen these before?"

Carrie thumbed through the neatly typed sheets. "Why yes, Mr. Hempstead. They are payrolls from the Mendocino mill."

"Miss McLean, did you type these lists?"

It struck Carrie as a very strange question. "Of course, sir."

"And these are exact copies of the list sent by the mill manager?"

"Yes, Mr. Hempstead." She wondered what he could possibly be suggesting.

"Tell me, please, Miss McLean, exactly how this payroll is handled."

"But you know the procedure, Mr. Hempstead."

"I want you to tell me exactly how you get the payroll from the mill and what you do with it." Mr. Hempstead wasn't shouting, but there was no mistaking his cold wrath.

She tried to answer calmly, explaining the procedure step by step. "Well, sir, the captain delivers the payroll list to Mr. Morgan, who gives it to me. I type a copy and give both back to Mr. Morgan. As I understand it, he gives them to you, and you give them back to him with the money after you go to the bank. Then I help him fill the individual pay envelopes."

"Just how do you help him, Miss McLean? Do you put the bills in the envelopes?"

"No, sir. I never handle the money." Carrie was frightened by his stern glare. "I never do that. Mr. Morgan fills the envelopes, while I check off the names and amounts on the list."

"Which list?" he demanded. "The handwritten one from the mill manager or this copy?"

Carrie hesitated, puzzled by his question. "The manager's list, as it happens."

"And the copy, the one you type? What do you do with that, Miss McLean?"

"Mr. Morgan always puts that in his file, sir. Since that is the copy with your signature, it is the one he keeps for a permanent record."

"And you never see the copy after you type it and return both lists to Mr. Morgan?"

"No, sir. I've no need of the copy for my work. Mr. Morgan is very careful of the payroll, sir. He always takes care of it personally."

"I see. Just one more question, Miss McLean. I have noticed that Mr. Morgan often escorts you home after work. Just what is your relationship to him?"

Carrie gasped. The question stunned her, and she had no idea how to answer. She suspected Roger would be angry if she told Mr. Hempstead they were engaged without discussing it with him. Besides, it might jeopardize her job, and she still owed Anna twenty-five dollars. Carrie fidgeted for a moment.

"Well, Miss McLean?"

"Mr. Morgan is kind enough to see me to my cable car sometimes," she hedged. "And we occasionally go out together." Carrie struggled to sound casual. "But we have no 'relationship' as you call it."

"Just casual acquaintances?" He didn't seem to believe her. She tried to sound more convincing. "Yes, sir, casual acquaintances."

"All right, Miss McLean. That is all for now. You may go." He followed her, almost pushing her out the door. "Mr. Morgan, I am afraid you will have to work late today. Will you please come into my office?"

Roger looked at Mr. Hempstead and then at Carrie's puzzled face. His hands clenched, she noticed, as he nodded to her. "Sorry I can't walk you home after all, Miss Carrie."

Chapter Seventeen

*I*t was eerie, Betsy. I felt as if he were accusing me of something."

"You, or Roger?"

"Oh, that's nonsense," Carrie retorted. "He trusts Roger like he would a son, and Roger wouldn't ever betray that trust."

Betsy idly turned the pages of *Vogue*. "How about this one?" she asked, pointing out a lavishly plumed millinery masterpiece.

"Betsy, come back to earth," Carrie protested. "I can't afford a hat like that."

"You only plan one trousseau, Carrie, and I can get the hat and the feathers at the Emporium for ten percent off and make it up myself."

"Maybe," Carrie shrugged, her mind still on the encounter of the day before. "It must just be some silly mistake. The mill manager probably got a name wrong or something. I'm sure Roger has it all cleared up already."

"Sure, Carrie."

"But they weren't at church this morning," Carrie said, feeling worried.

"Roger and his mother? Maybe Mrs. Morgan was feeling poorly. You said she's frail. Come on, Carrie. We have to pick out patterns so we can get to work. There's your wedding dress and my bridesmaid's dress and your going-away suit all to be made. Where's he taking you, by the way?"

"Where? Oh, you mean on a honeymoon? I don't know. Roger's not much interested in traveling. I'd like to go to Monterey maybe for a few days, and then stop off and introduce him to Papa and Anna. But we haven't talked much about it." Why did she suddenly think of dirigibles? "After all," she concluded, "the wedding is still five months off."

"Three fancy dresses and the other little things, of course," Betsy teased. "There'd be plenty of time if you didn't insist on working practically right up to the big day."

"I'm barely going to get Anna paid back as it is, Betsy. And Roger has a right to expect me to bring a nice hope chest to him, not debts."

"Just don't work yourself to death first."

"Don't worry about that," Carrie assured her. "I can push myself for this little while, with a whole life of comfort ahead of me."

"You're not marrying a Huntington or a Crocker, you know."

Carrie laughed. "And I wouldn't know how to behave with the likes of them anyhow. But the thought of that lovely big house, with all the modern conveniences—a gas range, Betsy! And gaslights and a telephone and a cleaning girl. After those years groveling at the Emporium and drudging at Fort Romie, doesn't it sound like a life of ease?"

"Yes, Carrie, it does. And you certainly deserve it. I just hope nothing happens to spoil it."

Roger was usually at work when Carrie arrived, but Monday morning his desk was empty. As Carrie let the door click behind her, Mr. Hempstead's office door opened. "Please come in here, Miss McLean," he demanded.

She stepped past him into the office, astonished to find it crowded. Mrs. Sloane, the founding partner's widow, sat in Mr. Hempstead's swivel chair. A tall, white-haired man Carrie recognized as Mr. Hempstead's attorney stood against the desk, facing the door. A dark, heavy-set stranger stood beside him. Carrie gasped as she saw a uniformed policeman step from behind the open door, push it closed, and take his post in front of it.

The attorney spoke. "Miss Caroline McLean, I believe?"

"Yes, sir. I'm Caroline McLean."

"Miss McLean, this is Inspector Durham, of the police department. He is going to ask you some questions concerning the Hempstead and Sloane payroll. I trust you will be cooperative." Carrie couldn't understand why a policeman could possibly want to question her. "Of course, sir. I will do all I can."

"I hope so." The stocky stranger stepped forward and confronted Carrie, waving some papers in her face. "I understand it is one of your duties to type these weekly payroll lists. Is that correct?"

"Yes, sir."

"From what do you copy them, Miss McLean?"

"From the lists the mill manager sends down, sir."

"How do you receive those lists?" he asked.

"They are delivered to Mr. Morgan, the bookkeeper. I get them from him."

Inspector Durham glared at her. "He hands you a handwritten list, and you type it?"

"Yes," Carrie answered.

"Exactly as it is given you?"

"Of course." Carrie felt very warm. She started to take off the fur wrap that she had not had time to remove when she came in.

"Miss McLean, where did you get that fur?" Mr. Hempstead asked. "You obviously didn't buy it on your salary."

"It was a gift," she said softly.

"From whom, Miss McLean?" the police inspector demanded.

"A friend," she stammered. "A friend gave it to me for Christmas."

"A gentleman friend, Miss McLean?" The inspector said it as if it were an accusation.

Carrie couldn't think of a good lie quickly enough. Besides, Roger wouldn't expect her to lie to the police. "From my fiancé."

"I didn't realize you were engaged to be married," Mr. Hempstead said coldly.

The inspector's musty tobacco smell almost sickened Carrie as he moved even closer. "And just who is your fiancé, Miss McLean? His name, please."

She drew a deep breath. It was then that the terrible truth began to dawn. "Mr. Morgan."

"Louder, Miss McLean, so we can all hear."

"Roger Morgan, sir."

Her inquisitor glowered in triumph. Mr. Hempstead and his attorney exchanged grimaces. Carrie heard the policeman behind her step forward. Only Mrs. Sloane's face showed any compassion.

The inspector continued to question her. "Are you aware, Miss McLean, that your intended is even now in the city jail?"

The stuffy little office began to spin around her. Carrie tried to focus on Mrs. Sloane's gentle, pitying face, avoiding the stony anger of her employer and the taunting smirk of the police inspector.

"Jail?" She gasped. "But, for what? Roger would never . . ."

"For padding the payroll, Miss McLean. He was caught red-handed and, since you, yourself, admit to typing these faked lists, it looks like you're going to join him there." The inspector seemed to be enjoying his triumph.

"Just a moment, officer," Mrs. Sloane interrupted. "Let me talk to the girl for a few minutes."

He stepped aside, and Mrs. Sloane motioned to Carrie to sit in the straight-backed chair beside her. "Carrie, did you do this because he asked you to?"

Her kindness gave permission to the tears Carrie had struggled to hold back. "Mrs. Sloane, I didn't do anything wrong."

"Tell me, Carrie, just what you did with the lists."

"Roger gave me the manager's list every Tuesday night and had me type a copy of it. Then I gave him back the original and the copy."

"And you never added names to it, names he gave you?"

"No, Mrs. Sloane, never."

"You gave both lists back to him and never saw them again?"

"No, not exactly." Carrie sniffed and daubed at her eyes. Mrs. Sloane's lips were firm, but her eyes were gentle. "Go on, Carrie. Tell us just what happened then."

Carrie swallowed hard and went on. "After Mr. Hempstead brought the money from the bank, Roger filled the pay envelopes. I always checked the names against the list."

"The same list, Carrie? This is very important. Was it the original list or the list you typed?"

"The handwritten one, Mrs. Sloane, as I told Mr. Hempstead on Saturday."

The attorney spoke then. "Miss McLean, did you ever, at any time, compare the list you checked against the pay envelopes with the copy you typed, the one signed by Mr. Hempstead?"

172

"No, sir. I knew I had copied it correctly. It never occurred to me to recheck it later."

"Carrie," Mrs. Sloane continued, stroking the lovely fox cape, "didn't you wonder how Mr. Morgan could afford such an expensive gift?"

"I . . . I guess I was flattered that he wanted me to have nice things. I assumed he was well paid, and he had an inheritance. His father died a couple of years ago, you know."

"Did he tell you his father had left him money?" Mrs. Sloane's voice was edged now with anger.

"I guess not, exactly, but that was the impression I had."

"What his father left, Miss McLean, were debts. He owed thousands of dollars," Mr. Hempstead informed her.

"But the house, the furniture . . ."

"All mortgaged to the hilt." The police inspector shrugged. "As if you didn't know." He motioned to the policeman who still stood behind Carrie. "I say take her in."

The attorney nodded, but Mr. Hempstead looked toward Mrs. Sloane, who shook her head. "Not yet. Carrie, look at me, my dear. Now tell me honestly, did you have any idea Mr. Morgan was stealing from the company all the time he was courting you and before?"

"Oh, no, Mrs. Sloane." How could Carrie make Mrs. Sloane believe her? "No, I swear it."

"The fur isn't the only thing he's given you, is it?"

"Some pearls. He said they had been his grandmother's. Books." More tears flowed. "A Bible. It was to be our family Bible, he said. And my engagement ring."

"Carrie, you will have to return them. You realize that." At least Mrs. Sloane seemed to believe her.

"Of course, immediately. I never want to see any of them or Roger ever again."

The uniformed policeman hovered. The inspector looked at him and at Mr. Hempstead. "I say it's just a good line, and I've heard lots of them, but it's up to you. Do we take her in or not?"

Mr. Hempstead and his attorney conferred briefly in a far corner of the office. The attorney spoke. "My client and I agree that the evidence against Miss McLean is less than convincing at present."

"You don't want to press charges?"

"We wish to pursue the investigation further and question Mr. Morgan in more detail before making that decision."

The policeman moved a few steps from Carrie, and she felt a hint of hope creep back into her heart. It was quickly buried, though, by the harsh words of his superior. "All right, Miss McLean, I guess you are free for now. But don't get any ideas about leaving town."

"As if I'd any place to go," Carrie sobbed, as she poured out the horrible story to Betsy that night.

"You could go home, Carrie."

"I can't go down there and face Papa and Anna, after all my talk about making a good life for myself, Betsy. Besides, the police would assume I was running away because I really did know what Roger was doing."

She clung to Betsy, wondering if anyone else in the world really believed her innocent. Betsy gave her a quick hug. "It must have been horrible having that policeman bring you home. I wonder what Mrs. Hurley thought."

"I'm afraid to imagine. He insisted on coming upstairs with me while I gathered the things." Carrie hadn't thought she had any tears left, but still another fell as she remembered the shame.

"Your engagement ring, too, of course."

"That isn't it," cried Carrie. "I meant it when I said I never wanted to see any of Roger's gifts again. Betsy, he took the watch Matt gave me. He wouldn't believe me. He was sure it was from Roger too."

"Oh, Carrie." Betsy stroked Carrie's hair as she might have a child's. "Oh, how could this happen to you? How could God let this happen to you?"

"At least I'm not going to blame God, Betsy. It was my own stupidity and, I guess, my greed. I should have known something was wrong."

Carrie left the boardinghouse at the usual time the next morning, not wanting Mrs. Hurley to know the truth. All day she walked the muddy streets in the cold January wind. She would not consider the possibility of going back to Fort Romie. She was not defeated yet.

She was a good typist, she told herself. Her work at Hempstead and Sloane had been entirely satisfactory, and there was no proof at all that she knew anything about Roger's theft. Surely Mr. Hempstead would be fair. Mrs. Sloane believed her. Maybe she would give her a letter of reference.

Carrie went home at the regular time, but Mrs. Hurley met her on the steps. "Carrie, I think you had better tell me what is going on."

"Why, Mrs. Hurley, nothing is wrong," she lied.

175

"I've got eyes, young lady." Mrs. Hurley's usually kind Irish brogue was harsh now. "Yesterday you came home early and with a police escort. Today, you walked out as if you were going to work, but a messenger came looking for you just after noon from Hempstead and Sloane. Now, out with it."

"A message from Mr. Hempstead? Please, Mrs. Hurley, let me see it."

"Here." She thrust it into Carrie's hand, and stood watching her, as Carrie opened it.

The note was cryptic. It said only that Carrie was to see him at his office as soon as possible. She tried to be optimistic. *Maybe I have been cleared*, she told herself. *Maybe he wants me back at work.*

Mrs. Hurley was waiting for her explanation. "Carrie, I like you, but I run a respectable boardinghouse. I can't have my girls being brought home by policemen. People talk."

She was bound to hear about Roger fairly soon anyhow, so Carrie told her, as calmly as she could, about his embezzlement. "But, Mrs. Hurley, I didn't know anything about it, anything at all."

"Poor child, of course ye didn't." She drew Carrie to her and patted her shoulder. "Men! We'd all be better off without them," she crooned.

"I'm certainly better off without Roger Morgan," Carrie agreed. "And Mr. Hempstead's note doesn't sound threatening. Maybe Roger has told them the truth, and Mr. Hempstead wants me back at work."

Carrie tried to believe that, as she walked down to the pier the next morning, but Mr. Hempstead still looked grim when he responded to her knock on his office door.

"Miss McLean, do come in. Won't you sit down?" The words were kind, but the voice was distant.

Carrie slid into the chair he indicated, and he sat, too, hands folded on his desk in front of him. "Miss McLean, the police notified my attorney yesterday that Mr. Morgan has made a statement."

Carrie's palms were cold and wet as she waited for him to continue.

He sighed. "Miss McLean, this is as difficult for me as it is for you. I, too, trusted that young man, and was taken in by him. He says that you were indeed innocent of his scheme."

A relieved sigh escaped Carrie's strained throat. "I'm sure that is good news to you, Miss McLean. And both Mrs. Sloane and I are inclined to believe your story. However, . . ."

He reached for a plain envelope on his desk. "However, under the circumstances, I feel it is necessary to terminate your employment with our firm."

He flipped the envelope with an index finger. "Obviously, it would be difficult to provide you with a reference. But Mrs. Sloane felt that, out of sympathy with your difficult position, we could offer you a week's severance pay."

He handed Carrie the envelope and stood. "Believe me, Miss McLean, I am very sorry this happened."

Chapter Eighteen

*C*arrie looked for a friendly
face, but the dozen or so
people beyond the courtroom railing were impassive,
except for Mrs. Morgan. She glared bitterly, as if she
blamed Carrie. *That's ridiculous*, Carrie thought. *Roger
started stealing before he even met me.* But Carrie still saw
hatred on Mrs. Morgan's lined face.

The prosecutor waved the sheaf of payroll sheets under
Carrie's nose. "Miss McLean, did you type these lists?"

"Yes," she whispered.

"Speak up," he pressed. "Did you?"

"Yes, sir. I did."

"From what did you type these lists, Miss McLean?"

"From the handwritten payroll we received from the
mill manager," Carrie responded.

"How did you get that payroll, Miss McLean?"

"From Mr. Morgan."

"From Mr. Morgan? Do you mean the defendant,
Roger Morgan?" the prosecutor demanded.

"Yes," she said.

"And after you typed them, what did you do with these lists, Miss McLean?"

Carrie looked at Roger. His eyes avoided hers, and she was glad. "After I typed the copy I gave both it and the original back to Mr. Morgan."

"You did not take them to Mr. Hempstead for his signature?" the prosecutor queried.

"No, sir. Mr. Morgan always checked them and then took them to Mr. Hempstead himself."

"Then you never saw these lists again after you typed them, Miss McLean?"

"No, sir. I mean, yes, sir. I did see the original again." Carrie struggled to keep her mind clear, though she was trembling with terror.

"You did?" The prosecutor stared down at her. "Would you explain why, Miss McLean?"

"After Mr. Hempstead brought the payroll money from the bank, Mr. Morgan and I filled the pay envelopes," Carrie explained. "Mr. Morgan used the typed list and put the money in as I checked off the name on the mill manager's list. Then Mr. Morgan put the manager's list and the envelopes into the box he gave to the ship's captain, and the captain delivered them to the mill manager."

"And the typed copy?"

"Mr. Morgan always put that in his own files," Carrie answered.

"Didn't you think it strange that you used the original list, rather than the copy with Mr. Hempstead's signature, to verify the pay envelopes, Miss McLean?"

Carrie fumbled with her handkerchief. "No, sir. Mr. Morgan used that list."

The prosecutor picked up a second stack of papers. "Are these the original lists, Miss McLean? You may compare them with the copies if you wish."

Carrie shuffled through them and recognized them as the ones she had been shown earlier, when the police had questioned her. "Yes, sir."

"And you say you never compared these with your typed copy after you prepared that copy?"

"No, sir. I checked them immediately after typing them and never had occasion to look at them closely after that, that is until the police showed them to me."

"Would you compare the two lists now, Miss McLean?"

He handed her the two sets of lists, and she looked again at the evidence she had been shown when the police first questioned her.

"Tell us, please, whether these typed copies agree with the originals."

"They did when I typed them," she insisted.

"Miss McLean, you have already testified that you typed the same names and that you did not see these copies again after you handed them to Mr. Morgan. Now, do these two sets of lists contain the same names?"

"Not exactly, sir." Roger's deception was obvious now, she realized. "The names from the manager's list are on the typed copy, in alphabetical order, but each copy also contains one or two additional names."

"Names you did not type, Miss McLean? How can you be so sure?"

"I did not add any name to the lists, sir," Carrie responded defensively. "And I always put the names in alphabetical order. The names that were added are out of order."

Roger glanced up from the table for just an instant. She was stunned by the pain in his pale eyes. He seemed to have aged ten years in the few weeks since they had planned their wedding.

"Miss McLean, to the best of your knowledge, did anyone other than yourself and Mr. Morgan have access to those payroll sheets between the time you typed them and the time Mr. Hempstead signed them?"

Roger stared at the table once more, but his mother looked at Carrie. Mrs. Morgan seemed to be pleading with Carrie to say something, anything, to help her son. Carrie had nothing to say but the truth. "No one, sir. The files were kept locked, and as far as I know Mr. Morgan and Mr. Hempstead had the only keys."

"Now, Miss McLean, you have told us that Mr. Morgan had access to these two lists. Did he not also have ready access to your typewriting machine?"

"I never saw him use it, sir."

"But he could have used it without your knowing about it? He was regularly in the office when you were not. Isn't that correct?"

Carrie remembered how Roger always came to work early. She had even bragged to Betsy about how dedicated he was to the company. "He was nearly always in the office when I arrived in the morning."

"Thank you, Miss McLean. I have just one more question. Miss McLean, I remind you that you are under oath. Do you swear, under oath, that the original and the copy you typed and handed to Mr. Morgan were identical in every way and that at no time did you alter either original or copy?"

"Yes, sir. I swear I never changed either one."

"That is all, Miss McLean. Your Honor, I have no further questions."

Roger spoke a few words to his attorney, who then spoke to the judge. "We have no questions for this witness, Your Honor."

The next morning as Carrie sat and watched Betsy dress for work, the sag of her heart matched that of the cheap mattress. "Shouldn't you be getting dressed, Carrie?" Betsy asked. "You want to be at the agency early, don't you?"

"I'm just so exhausted from yesterday, Betsy. Besides, what's the use? I've been there first thing every morning for weeks. I've been to twenty offices. It's always the same thing. 'And why did you leave Hempstead and Sloane, Miss McLean?' If I tell the truth they won't take a chance on me, and if I lie they ask for a reference."

"You didn't do anything wrong, Carrie, and lots of people will believe you. You just haven't found the right one yet. You're really good at typewriting. You have the letter from the school that says so."

"Lots of girls can use a typewriter now. And most of them weren't engaged to an embezzler."

"Have you tried not saying anything at all about Hempstead and Sloane?" Betsy suggested. "You know, like saying you went back to Soledad for a while after you took the typewriting course or something."

"I've thought about it, Bets, but I'm just not a good liar." Still, she had to do something, Carrie thought, as she waited later at the employment agency for another interview. It had been two months since she'd been discharged, and her meager savings were nearly gone.

"Miss McLean."

The receptionist beckoned, and Carrie hurried to the desk, expecting a slip of paper with the name and address of another possible employer.

"Miss McLean, Mr. Brown wishes to see you in his office."

She seemed to be snickering, but Carrie brushed the feeling aside, wondering why the agency owner could possibly want to see her again. Mr. Brown stood as she entered his office. He didn't ask her to sit, and his thin face was angry. A newspaper lay on his desk.

"Miss McLean, I assume you are aware of the contents of this." He picked the paper up and slapped it back onto the desk.

Carrie wasn't, but she could guess from his tone. "No, sir. I haven't seen the morning paper."

"You should. You will find it most interesting."

He almost threw the tabloid at her. It was folded open, and a heading in the middle of the page leaped at her. "Bookkeeper Convicted in Payroll Fraud."

"Miss McLean, we demand that our girls be above reproach." Mr. Hempstead had at least tried to sound kind, but Mr. Brown snarled. "Obviously, you cannot meet that qualification. This agency will no longer refer you, nor, I assure you, will any other respectable employment service."

For the moment Carrie was too angry for tears, but by the time she reached the boardinghouse she was fighting back her sobs. Mrs. Hurley met her in the hall. A newspaper lay on the table, and she hurriedly slipped it into a drawer.

"My dear," she said, opening her arms to Carrie. "Carrie, they had no right to use your name. You weren't charged with any crime."

"Oh, Mrs. Hurley, what can I do? The agency won't recommend me. I'll never be able to find work."

"There, now. The paper even says that Roger himself insisted you weren't involved. This will blow over."

"But, Mrs. Hurley, my savings are nearly gone. I've no money."

"What about your family, Carrie? They are doing pretty well now, aren't they?"

"Not well enough to lend to me. Any cash they get has to go into the farm," Carrie explained. *Besides,* she thought, *how could I ever admit to them what a mess I've made of my life?*

Betsy made the same suggestion that evening. "I can manage the rent for both of us for a few weeks, Carrie, but . . ."

"Of course you can't, Betsy. That would take every cent you make. You wouldn't even have carfare left."

"Well, for a little while I could. But maybe it would be best for you to go back to Soledad."

"Never!"

"Was it really that bad?"

185

"It isn't that. I could stand the dust and the fog and the wind. But to tell Papa and Anna what a fool I've been . . ."

"You're going to have to tell them the truth sooner or later," Betsy reminded her. "They think you're getting married in June."

"No. I already wrote that I'd broken my engagement. I told them I was afraid Roger was too attached to his mother."

"You don't lie, but you use the truth interestingly." Betsy smiled. "But they love you, Carrie. They'd understand how he used you."

"I let him use me. Betsy, anyone with a grain of sense would have known Roger couldn't afford to live the way he did on his salary. The house, the nice furniture, the hired girl—and the things he gave me. He couldn't have gotten that much money honestly, and I should have known it."

"You thought he'd inherited the house. You had no way of knowing it was mortgaged. Why, even his mother didn't guess what was going on."

"I was stupid. I certainly should have known the pay envelopes should be checked against the same copy Mr. Hempstead signed."

"Why should you have known, Carrie? You aren't a bookkeeper, and you never worked in any other office. How would you know how things like that should be done?"

"If I hadn't been so wrapped up in how 'respectable' Roger was, and how nice it would be to be the wife of a 'substantial businessman,' I wouldn't have been taken in."

"I guess I understand how you feel about telling your folks," Betsy conceded. "But you'll just have to find some kind of a job."

Carrie stared at the floor for a few minutes as Betsy unpinned her long hair and began to brush it. "You know," Betsy said suddenly, "Mr. Samuels at the Emporium knows you're honest. I'll bet he'd take you back."

Carrie thought of the hours and hours standing behind the counter, smiling while her back and legs and feet screamed with exhaustion. She remembered the demands and complaints of the customers. Then she thought of the few coins left in her purse. "Do you really think he might, Betsy?"

Betsy was late the next night, and supper was on the table when she rushed in, but she gave Carrie's hand a quick squeeze as she slid into her chair. Immediately after supper she dragged Carrie up to their room. "Carrie," she puffed. "I didn't even have to broach the subject with Mr. Samuels. He came up to me as I was going to lunch and asked how you were doing. He'd seen the story in the paper."

"Hasn't everyone?"

"But, Carrie, he was really concerned. He said he couldn't believe you'd ever steal anything."

It was good to hear that someone believed her, especially Mr. Samuels, who, as the Emporium's sternest floorwalker, had always terrified all his girls.

Betsy chattered on. "Mr. Samuels says one of the girls in yardage is quitting next week to get married, and if you'll come in tomorrow and talk to him, he thinks he can get you the job."

As Carrie dressed the next morning to go to the store, she recalled the first time she had gone to the Emporium looking for a job. She had been so excited then. She was sixteen and thrilled with the idea of working amidst fashionable clothes and meeting the people who shopped at the city's finest store. Now she was desperate. She had to have work, and the drudgery of the yard goods department promised nothing more than a livelihood.

"But I just have to have this job, Lord," she prayed, as she walked downtown. "If you're there, if you're listening, if you care at all what happens to me, let me get this job."

Chapter Nineteen

*C*arrie, you can't survive on just a cup of tea for lunch every day. Here." Betsy shoved her bread plate toward Carrie. "At least eat a slice of my bread."

The lunch counter was crowded, as always. "No, Betsy, I'm not going to take any of your lunch. It's all right, really. I'm not that hungry, what with Mrs. Hurley's good breakfast and dinner." Carrie pushed the bread back to her. "But I think I'll skip the tea tomorrow too."

"Carrie, you're not that strapped for money. Anna isn't pushing you on the loan, is she?"

"Oh my, no, Bets. I do want to get her paid back though. And I can, nearly as quickly as I'd planned, by cutting just a few corners."

"Well, I think your cup of midday tea is just too much to give up."

Carrie laughed as she saw the waitress glance their way again. "It isn't the price of the tea. It's that waitress! Can't you tell what she thinks of my taking up a stool at the counter for nothing but a cup of tea? So I think I'll just take a breath of fresh air on my lunch period for a few days."

"I'd think being on your feet ten hours a day would be enough reason to sit for half an hour at noon." Betsy winced. "It sure is for me."

"It's not really as bad as I remembered, Betsy. Why, sitting at the typewriter all day was tiring too."

"It paid better. And you got off earlier. Do you think you'll be able to get another office job in a little while?"

"Sure I will." Carrie wished she were as confident as she tried to sound. "People will forget about Roger soon. Meantime, I'm making enough to live on and still send Anna her five dollars a month. Two more months and I'll be out of debt. Then, when I've put aside a few dollars, I'll go to another agency. This time I'll explain that I went back to Soledad to help my father for a while after I finished the typewriting course."

They hurried back to the store, Betsy to ladies' gloves and Carrie to yard goods. She recognized the customer who was waiting. She was a member of the church Carrie had attended with Roger and his mother.

"Good afternoon, Mrs. Smythe."

The customer stared at Carrie for a few moments, then lifted her eyebrows as she remembered who Carrie was. "Well, Miss McLean," she snorted. "So you've come down to selling yardage."

Carrie pretended not to notice the insult as she measured out the six yards of dimity the woman requested. Mrs. Smythe handed her a five dollar gold piece, and Carrie reached into the cashbox for change.

190

She counted the small change and four dollar bills into her hand, and Mrs. Smythe walked away with the package but turned back, almost immediately. "Miss McLean," she demanded loudly. "Where is your supervisor?"

Mr. Samuels must have heard her, because he appeared in an instant. "Sir, this girl, this thief in your employ, just stole five dollars from me."

Mr. Samuels looked at Carrie. She could only shake her head, bewildered. "No, sir. I didn't."

"I gave her a ten dollar gold piece to pay for six yards of dimity, and she gave me change for only five dollars." She was accusing Carrie in such a piercing tone that Carrie felt the whole store full of people must be watching. "But then, what do you expect when you employ known criminals?"

"Now, now," Mr. Samuels soothed. "Let's all go into the office and talk this over. I'm sure it's a simple misunderstanding."

He picked up Carrie's cashbox and pushed her ahead of him into the manager's office.

Carrie felt as helpless as she had when she'd been questioned about Roger's embezzlement. Mrs. Smythe repeated her charge, and Mr. Samuels demanded an answer.

"Mr. Samuels, I am certain Mrs. Smythe gave me a five dollar gold piece, not ten dollars. And I gave her four twenty-two in change."

"She gave me four twenty-two all right, but she owes me another five dollars."

Mr. Samuels emptied the contents of the cashbox onto the desk. There were several five dollar pieces, but there was one ten dollar piece as well. "I remember a customer giving me that just before lunchtime, Mr. Samuels. She bought ten yards of ivory satin. I remember, because she said it was for her daughter's wedding dress."

"A likely story." Mrs. Smythe sounded as if she really believed she'd given Carrie ten dollars. If there had been two ten dollar gold pieces in the box, Carrie might have believed her too. "She stole, and she's lying about it, just as she plotted to rob Hempstead and Sloane, trapped poor Roger Morgan into helping her, and then managed to make him take all the blame. You did know about that, didn't you?"

Mr. Samuels shifted his weight from one foot to the other. "Mrs. Smythe, I was aware Miss McLean had been, ah, involved, in an unfortunate episode in her last position." He glared at Carrie. "Miss McLean, we were willing to give you a second chance because you had appeared to be a trustworthy employee in the past and assured us you were innocent in the recent matter. You still have a chance to make good here. Are you absolutely certain Mrs. Smythe gave you only five dollars?"

Carrie knew immediately what he was saying. He meant she could give Mrs. Smythe the five dollars and apologize without losing her job. She thought about it, then spoke carefully. "Mr. Samuels, I understand what you want, but I can't do it. I know where that ten dollar gold piece came from, and there is no other. If I said I was wrong, you would still think I was a thief, wouldn't you?"

"Miss McLean, what I think is not really at issue. The Emporium has an impeccable reputation to maintain, and if Mrs. Smythe says she gave you ten dollars, she gave you ten dollars." He took one of the five dollar coins from the pile on the desk and handed it to her. "Mrs. Smythe, I am very sorry this happened. Please accept my apology, and do call again. I assure you this will not happen a second time."

She dropped the coin into her purse. "It most certainly will not," she sneered. "For if you do not discharge this wanton thief immediately, I shall insist that your superior do so."

Mr. Samuels riveted his eyes on the pile of money. "Miss McLean, you realize that this is a matter of your word against that of the customer, and you know that the customer is always right. I am afraid I have no choice."

"But, Mr. Samuels, you can look in my purse. I don't have that much money."

"Miss McLean, I do not intend to argue the matter. Please collect your things and leave."

"But I didn't take the money."

Mrs. Smythe still stood by the door glowering. "Mr. Samuels, we both know that the manager would not accept the word of a shop girl and accused thief over that of a respectable community member and good customer."

"Mr. Samuels, I need this job," Carrie pleaded.

"Miss McLean, that is your misfortune."

"My week's pay?" Carrie murmured. "It is Friday, and . . ."

"It should just about cover the five dollar shortage, Miss McLean. If there is anything coming to you, we will send it to your home address."

Mrs. Smythe swept through the door he held for her. He bowed to her and then pulled himself up to his full five-foot-four and waved Carrie past. "Well," he muttered, more to himself than to her, "I did all I could. I took a chance on you, and I just hope I don't lose my position over it."

Carrie had two dollars set aside for Anna. That wasn't even enough to pay Mrs. Hurley her room and board.

"I can pay for both of us for a few weeks, Carrie. Honest, I don't mind," Betsy assured her. "You'd do the same for me."

"Not likely. With my luck I'd never have the means."

"Carrie, that's all it is, a streak of bad luck. You never stole from Hempstead and Sloane, and you never stole from this Smythe woman. She just did it for spite."

"Maybe she really thought I did try to cheat her. Mrs. Morgan must have told her those lies about my getting Roger into trouble. Betsy, how could she? He started padding that payroll right after his father died and left all those debts. That was a year, or more, before I went to work there."

"She's his mother, Carrie. She can't blame him or herself, so she has to find someone else. You just happened to be handy."

"And I just happened to be handy today. Now I've no job, no money. I owe Anna, and I owe you. What in the world am I going to do?"

"You're going to get a good night's sleep and take the weekend off." Betsy forced a laugh. "I wish I didn't have to face the Saturday mob tomorrow morning myself."

Carrie trudged the city streets searching for work—the same bustling streets she had longed for during the years in Soledad. Women darted from shop to shop choosing spring finery. Fruit bins and flower carts brightened every corner of Union Square. *Will that be my next occupation?* Carrie wondered, glancing at the bunched blossoms. She doubted she could pay the rent at Mrs. Hurley's by selling flowers.

The employment agents shook their heads. "Sorry, Miss McLean, but we've plenty of girls with good references. Two dismissals, even if you were innocent . . ."

She tried lying about the past year, saying she had spent it with her family. But that brought new questions. "Why did you come back to the city anyhow? Perhaps you should have stayed in, where is it, Soledad, wherever that is, where people know you."

Why did I come here? Carrie asked herself. It was a sunny May day, and she sat alone watching the ocean waves break against the rocks below Mr. Sutro's fancy bathhouse. *Why wasn't I content to stay in Soledad? Why did I leave just when things were beginning to go well there?*

She was jarred from her self-pity by the jangle of a tambourine. *Maybe that was why I left.* She chuckled as she watched the little Salvation Army band assembling near the entrance to the baths, the lassies in their red- and gold-trimmed bonnets, the men in the familiar military-type navy uniforms. There was a cornet, a trombone, and

195

the tambourines, of course. The lusty, if not harmonic voices rang out, "Whate'er I do, Where'er I be, Still 'tis God's hand that leadeth me."

"He's done a great job so far! He's led me straight to the gutter!" Carrie hadn't meant to say it out loud and certainly not loud enough to be heard by a Salvation Army lassie hustling past on her way to the street meeting.

"Has he, now?" the girl questioned, settling down on the rock beside Carrie. The last thing Carrie wanted was some goody-goody Army lassie patting her hand and telling her the Lord would work things out. But the girl's warm voice, with its hint of a brogue, warmed Carrie. "You look in need of a friend."

"Friends I've got, thank God," Carrie muttered, thinking of Betsy and her open-handed loyalty. "Friends, but little else."

"With friends I find you need little else."

"That sounds good," Carrie snapped, "but right now I need a job more."

The girl's eyes swept Carrie from head to toe. "So that should be little trouble. You're young, healthy, neat in appearance, obviously bright."

"And everybody in San Francisco thinks I'm a thief," Carrie blurted.

Her confession didn't seem to faze her new friend. "Are you?" the girl asked matter-of-factly.

"I'm not. Truly I'm not, but that doesn't seem to matter." Carrie found herself pouring out the whole story to the smiling stranger. "And so," she concluded, "I came up here to earn my way. I just wanted to work hard, be honest, mind my own business, and get decent pay for my

196

efforts. And this is what I've gotten for it. This is where your just and loving God has led me."

"You do believe in God, though, don't you?" she prodded gently.

"Of course! I'm as good a Christian as most people." Carrie expected the girl to argue, but she just sat, smiling, watching the waves. "I am," Carrie insisted. "I tell the truth. I don't steal, whatever they all say. I go to church. I pray."

"You work, and you expect your boss to pay you. You go to church and say your prayers, and you expect God to pay you, right?"

"Well . . ." Carrie shrugged. "Isn't that just about it? Except that God is supposed to be fair. He's not supposed to punish us for things we didn't do."

"Like your employers did?"

"Yes, like my employers. Where was God when they were firing me without cause? Oh, I know what you're going to say. 'We have to have faith.' Well, I know all about faith."

The Salvation Army lassie smiled. "It seems to work for me."

"Does it? How much do you know about Fort Romie, Commander Booth-Tucker's great experiment? Do you know people starved, literally starved, trying to wrench a living from that baked adobe, trying to squeeze water from the quicksand of that riverbed?"

"But you said yourself that your father is doing well now," the girl reminded her.

"No thanks to God," Carrie snapped. "Oh, Papa thanks God, but it was Anna's money that saved him— Anna's and my brother Rob's."

"We never claimed that God didn't use people," the lassie explained. "In fact, that's the whole idea behind the Salvation Army, that we let him use us."

"Then there's Matt," Carrie reflected. "Let me tell you about Matt. Faith! You never saw faith like Matt's. God's going to give him a farm. He was positive. He'd worked like a slave all his life. He was saved in an Army meeting at Fort Romie, and he spent all his spare time after that helping the colonists with their farms. Went to work at Spreckles Sugar Mill to save enough money for that farm he knew God meant him to have."

Carrie hadn't let herself think of Matt for a long time. But now, as she told this stranger about his obsession, she remembered his shock of copper hair, the broad grin under his handlebar mustache, and his deep, cool blue eyes. And she remembered his confidence and his promises. "Matt Hanlon will tell you God is his partner. Well, let me tell you, God is a partner in a losing enterprise. Matt lost everything he'd saved in the drought last year."

"Everything, or his savings?" Carrie's new friend prodded.

"What else did he have but his savings?"

"Faith, hope, dreams. Did he lose those too?"

Carrie recalled the day she'd told Matt she was leaving Fort Romie, the day he'd coldly wished her luck. "The last time I saw him he'd stopped talking about his dream. I haven't heard from him since I came here."

The Salvation Army band had finished its street meeting without Carrie's companion. "I must go on to the evening service, Carrie. But will you think about something for a little while? You've tried to win your dream by your own efforts, and you're not doing too well. If you still want a job, come to corps headquarters Monday morning and we'll see what we can do. But, in the meantime, why don't you think about trying life God's way? Remember, he can only lead you when you're willing to follow."

She left, and Carrie was alone again with the waves. The girl was right about one thing. Carrie's way hadn't worked. But then, neither had God's. *Where is Matt now?* she wondered. She hoped, somehow, with or without God's help, that he had his farm and a good girl to share it with him.

The sun was setting as Carrie started the long walk back to Mrs. Hurley's boardinghouse. *Mother told me,* she recalled, *that I should marry a realist.* "Ha," she sputtered. "Mother would have approved of Roger."

Then, for a few blocks, she thought about Papa's dreams. *His dreams failed Mother, and he regretted that sincerely, but now Papa's dreams seemed to be coming true. And, if Anna's money had made the difference, how can I be so sure God didn't send Anna? Papa thought so. So, come to think of it, did Anna.*

Stars began to appear in the twilight sky as Carrie trudged up the hill. To the north she could make out the shadows of Angel Island and rocky little Alcatraz in the moonlight. *I decided to come back to the city and be a career woman, and I decided, coolly and dispassionately, to marry Roger,* Carrie admitted to herself. *The Salvation Army lassie was right. My way hasn't worked too well, has it?*

There was a ring around the moon, and Carrie remembered the old saying. *A ring around the moon means rain,* she thought. The man in the moon grinned at her, and she heard Matt's voice. "There are willows, and where willows grow there's water." That wasn't blind faith. It was trust in a promise. And Matt's farm—was that a promise too?

Carrie trudged back downhill, into the Hayes Valley. Lights twinkled in the windows of the frame cottages as she walked past. She thought of the families within— fathers, mothers, and children building lives together in love. She shivered in the evening breeze, and the remembrance of Matt's touch warmed her.

The lights blurred in the tears that filled her eyes. Suddenly she wanted Matt's touch again, and she wanted to share his dream.

A shaft of moonlight fell across the steps of a church, and she followed it inside. Could she have been wrong? If her logic and her common sense had been so false, could the dreams and the faith be reality?

Once inside, Carrie told herself that she was only sitting down to rest. It was a very long walk from the beach back to Mrs. Hurley's.

The moonlight peeped through a stained-glass window and touched a cross at the front of the sanctuary. *He was the most perfect man that ever lived*, Carrie thought, *and they killed him. God isn't fair!*

The absurdity of it struck her. God, unfair, and to God, to himself. Hadn't she heard something from the Bible about God's wisdom being foolishness to man, or was it man's wisdom being foolishness to God? Her wisdom looked foolish even to her right then. Maybe it was time to try God's way.

She slipped to her knees and said the words aloud. "Lord, I don't know where to turn. I've tried to do right, to live right. But I've tried to do it on my own, and I've made a real mess out of things." It was true, but it didn't sound much like a prayer.

"Lord, I'm not very good at asking for help. But I don't seem to be very good at getting along without help either. I do believe in you, and I want to trust you like Matt does. I don't know where to go or what to do. Somebody in the Bible prayed once and said, 'I believe; help my unbelief.' I guess that's what I want to pray, too, Lord. I want to follow you, but I don't know how. Help me to believe. Teach me to trust. Lord, if you do care what I do with my life, please tell me what to do."

Chapter Twenty

*C*arrie knelt in the dark church for a long time. She argued with God for a while. She told him she'd tried, but finally she admitted she'd failed.

"My best isn't enough, Lord. I need you," she confessed, "and not just to save me from hell. I can't make my own success in this life, either." At last, beyond despair, she begged, "Please, Lord, tell me what you want me to do." And then, for the first time in her life, she listened.

There were no bells ringing, no messages written by the moonbeams. But as Carrie left the church and walked down the empty streets toward Mrs. Hurley's boarding-house, she knew the Lord would work things out. She knew, and at last she understood how Matt knew about his farm.

A lamp still burned in Mrs. Hurley's window, and Carrie was startled to find her and Betsy waiting in the parlor. "Carrie McLean, where in the world have you been to this hour?" Mrs. Hurley demanded.

"Yes, Carrie," Betsy echoed. "We've been so worried about you."

"Walking mostly," Carrie answered absently.

"Walking until after midnight?" Mrs. Hurley pulled Carrie down onto the sofa beside her.

"I'm sorry I worried you. I went out to the beach to think about what to do next. I met someone out there, and we talked for a while."

"Someone you knew, Carrie?" Betsy interrupted. "Did you get a job?"

"Not exactly. It was a Salvation Army lassie, actually."

Mrs. Hurley, good Irish Catholic that she was, snorted, but Betsy patted Carrie's hand. "Maybe they can help, Carrie. Did she say they might help you get a job?"

"As a matter of fact, she did suggest I come by corps headquarters on Monday."

"But surely you didn't talk to her until this hour, Carrie. Their meetings can't last so long," Mrs. Hurley protested.

"No, Mrs. Hurley. I didn't go to the meeting with her anyhow. She said some other things I needed to think over, so I've been walking and sitting." Carrie hesitated, not knowing how to explain what had happened. "And praying."

"Well, that never hurt anyone, anyhow," the older woman said. "Now, I've some soup on the stove, and you must be starved."

Mrs. Hurley ladled out a bowl of steaming clam chowder and poured coffee for herself and Betsy. "Oh, I nearly forgot." Betsy dashed out and returned with an envelope in her hand. "You got a letter from Anna today."

A shadow of doubt invaded Carrie's calm as she recalled her debt to her stepmother, but she opened the letter eagerly.

Anna wrote brightly, just as she was. Carrie smiled at her reports of the boys' dirty legs sticking out of last year's too-short knickers. She'd used some egg money for serge, she said, and was busy with sewing.

She went on about the Svensen's new team, and about new colonists coming to Fort Romie. This time, she explained, the land was being sold mostly to local people, people who knew the valley and who knew farming. *People like Matt*, Carrie thought, but Anna didn't mention him.

Then, as Carrie read the last paragraph, she began to cry.

"Oh, Carrie, is something wrong at home?" Betsy asked.

"Oh, no! Oh my, no. Betsy, she's going to have a baby. Anna and Papa are having a baby." Carrie brushed a tear of joy from her cheek. "Isn't it wonderful? She sounds so happy about it."

"That's great, Carrie. When?"

"She says she didn't write sooner because she didn't want me worrying about her when I was busy planning my wedding, but the baby should be born the end of next month. And she says, 'I know you can't leave your job, but it would be so nice if you could be here for my confinement.'"

"They think you are still working for Hempstead and Sloane, don't they?"

"Yes, Betsy. I just never figured out how to tell them what happened." Carrie slapped the letter idly against her hand. "I wonder . . ."

"You're going home, young lady." Mrs. Hurley shook a motherly finger in Carrie's face. "And it's happy I am for you."

"It does make the perfect excuse, Carrie," Betsy concurred. "And by the time Anna doesn't need you any more, maybe things will have settled down here."

Carrie nodded. "I think, maybe, this is the answer to my prayer. But I'm going to sleep on it and ask the Lord. This time I'm going to do it his way."

"I'm afraid I'm a little new at this," Carrie explained on Monday morning to her new friend, whose name turned out to be Kate. "I always figured religion was for Sunday, and salvation for heaven."

Kate nodded. "Jesus promised to supply all our needs. We, in his Army, do our best to carry out his wishes. Now, you need a job, right?"

"Well, maybe. But after I talked to you I stopped at a church to pray. I promised that from now on I would try to do what God wanted, instead of what I thought was best. And when I got back to the boardinghouse there was a letter from my stepmother. She is expecting a baby next month and said she wished I could be there."

"Well," Kate smiled. "You can."

"And I want to be, Kate. But isn't that too easy?"

"What do you mean, too easy?"

206

"When I told God I would do what he wanted, I expected something hard," Carrie confessed. "I guess I thought I should do something humble and good. How can I know whether the letter from Anna was an answer to my prayer or another temptation to work things out my way?"

"What makes you think going home will be easy, Carrie?"

Carrie laughed. "If you knew Anna, you'd understand. She's not only my stepmother. She's a very good friend. She's loving, tender, generous. And Papa, well, Papa's stern sometimes, but his heart is as big as that valley he loves so much."

"If you went, would you tell them why?"

Carrie hadn't really thought of that, and she didn't answer right away.

"You wouldn't have to, of course. You could just say you quit your job to help Anna."

"No, Kate, I couldn't. I'd have to tell them." Carrie drew a deep breath. "I'd have to admit my failure. And you're right. That would be the hardest thing I've ever done in my life."

"Carrie, I meant what I said about our helping you get a job," Kate assured her. "We do have contacts, and we could almost certainly find someone willing to give you another chance. But I don't think that is God's will for you right now. Do you?"

Carrie took the Tuesday train south. As the miles clattered past she tried not to think about where she would go after the baby came and Anna was strong again. *The Lord will show me that when the time comes*, she told herself.

A more immediate problem was how she would explain her sudden appearance, and how and when she would tell them that she had been taken in by Roger and accused of theft. *I'll just tell them I missed them, and couldn't bear to stay away, especially when Anna needed me*, she resolved. *Then later there will be a chance.* She hoped there wouldn't be, but she knew. She had had to confess her failure to God, and she would have to confess it to Anna and to her father. *Well*, she reminded herself, *God forgave me. And so will Papa and Anna.*

And Matt? Carrie tried not to think about Matt, but as the small towns of the San Francisco Peninsula gave way to the open fields of the Santa Clara Valley, in her mind Anna's glow and Sam's grin gave way to Matt's piercing stare.

When I rejected his dreams, I rejected him, she realized. *He was so persistent for a while. That New Year's Eve he was absolutely sure he could change my mind, and he almost did. But then he lost all his savings during the drought. He lost everything. I left*, Carrie thought, *and he just let me go.*

Carrie hadn't seen his eyes when she said good-bye. He'd scuffed his feet in the barren adobe and peered at the rising dust as he wished her luck. How could she tell Matt that she'd always loved him and that now she understood him too?

Anna's letters had never once mentioned his name. "He's gone," Carrie muttered. "Left the valley and abandoned his dream. And it was my fault."

Two years before, in the one good spring Carrie had seen there, the Salinas Valley had been green, but she was completely unprepared for the vista before her as the train chugged down the pass toward Salinas City. Lush pastures rolled down the gentle slopes of the Gabilan Range to the east, which were dotted with dazzling mustard in bloom. Plump cattle stood knee-deep already in the luxurious spring grass, browsing contentedly.

Along the railroad tracks the rangeland gave way to neatly plowed and planted fields, and the rich black soil was punctuated with ordered rows of young sugar beets. Carrie discovered she had learned more farm lore than she thought as she identified wheat, alfalfa, and corn. Near each scattered farmhouse a kitchen garden bore promise of fresh vegetables soon.

Carrie noticed another crop too. Many of those scattered farmhouses stood in the lee of bright new windmills and redwood water tanks. This time there really was hope that the crops would stay green. *There will be a harvest this year*, she realized, *and the next, and the next*.

Only twenty-five more miles, she calculated, as the train pulled out of Salinas City. She ticked off the little farming towns: first Chualar, then Gonzales. At last she stood on the platform in Soledad and recalled the first time she had stood there. They had such high hopes then, despite the barren soil and hot, dry wind. Now the valley was bright with growing things, and the breeze was fresh.

Again, no one was there to meet her, but this time no one was expecting her. She could have waited for someone she knew to come along and offer her a ride, but she decided to leave her trunk at the station and walk.

The river was still high, but Carrie found a ferry tied to a willow. She vaguely remembered the old man who answered her call for a ferryman.

He frowned as he peered at her through his spectacles. Then he pushed them onto his forehead. "Carrie! Carrie McLean, isn't it? Come home to help when the wee one arrives?"

"That's right," she answered. "Anna wrote that she'd like me to come, and I was homesick anyhow."

He helped her onto the opposite bank and tied his raft to await a return passenger. Carrie trudged up the rutted roadway, sniffing the sweetness of grass, trees, and moist soil. And she listened. She had forgotten the sounds of the country—the coo of the quail, the click of a grasshopper, the whish of the wind.

The cottage door stood open, and the toasty smell of fresh bread drifted out. Carrie tiptoed inside. "Anybody home?" she queried.

A pan clattered to the floor as Anna turned away from the loaves cooling on the kitchen table. "Carrie! Carrie, honey, whatever are you doing here?" she cried, floury arms outstretched in welcome. "You didn't give up your good job and come down here because you thought I needed you?"

"Anna." Carrie buried her face in Anna's apron bib for a moment. "Oh, Anna, I came home because I wanted to. You just gave me an excuse." Carrie stood back to look at her and at the familiar kitchen.

"Don't look too close, Carrie. I'm a big, clumsy ox." She laughed, and tossed her head. "But I'm a happy ox, Carrie, and the more so seeing you, if you really came home because you wanted to."

"Why else?" Carrie assured her. "Now, sit down while I take care of that bread. You must be exhausted, even if you don't look it."

Carrie took the last of the bread from the oven and sat down opposite Anna.

"It was the young man, wasn't it, Carrie? Your letters sounded so happy until you wrote of breaking the engagement. Since then I've read what your letters didn't say. He hurt you, didn't he?"

"Anna, I really don't want to talk about it yet. I'll tell you everything later, I promise."

"Any time. I'm here to listen whenever you want to tell me."

"I know, but now I want to hear about you and Papa and the boys. You look so well, and the valley is so green. I've never seen it like this."

"Yes, it's been a good winter. We've had plenty of grass for the cows since January, and we've had milk and butter enough to keep and to sell. The chickens have been laying well. The boys still trap rabbits, and we've raised a good litter of piglets too. Butchered the first one just last week. Carrie, this is how the valley is, usually. It was just the few bad years, only two dry years, really. But so many didn't make it through."

"The whole Fort Romie Colony failed, except for Papa, and he'd not have made it without you," Carrie said.

"That's not quite true. Your papa's stubborn. It would have been harder, but I think he'd have made it. It's me that had given up."

"Not really. You had Eric to think about, and you do have family in Denmark."

"But now I have family here. I love your Papa and all our sons. I love you, Carrie, though at your age you'd better not take to calling me Mama. And now this little one." She stroked her swollen stomach. "It is so good to feel new life growing within you. You'll know, Carrie, one of these days."

Sam and the boys were even more surprised to see her than Anna had been. They chattered all through supper. Then the boys insisted on showing Carrie their calf and the garden they'd planted for Anna "'cause she didn't feel like it this year."

As they went back inside, Carrie congratulated the boys on the garden. "Matt helped us a lot," Tim volunteered.

"Oh." She struggled to keep her voice casual. "Then Matt is still around."

"Isn't it your bedtime, Timmy?" Anna interrupted quickly. "And Carrie promised to help me with the dishes."

"How is Matt?" Carrie persisted. "You never mentioned him in your letters. I thought maybe he'd left the valley."

"Did, for a while," Sam offered. "But he got himself a stake working over Fresno way and turned up here again when the rains started. Fact is, he's got himself . . ."

"Sam, Carrie's going to need a place to sleep tonight," Anna burst in. "Maybe you'd better make up a bedroll in the other room for yourself for the time being, and she can sleep out here with me."

"No, Papa, you mustn't give up your bed," Carrie protested. "I'll curl up in the boys' room. I don't mind."

"No, Carrie," Anna insisted. "You sleep out here with me tonight, and tomorrow we'll work out something better."

Chapter Twenty-One

*C*arrie told Anna everything on Friday afternoon as they drove into Soledad for Carrie's trunk. "I thought I could make it on my own, Anna. I had all the answers. And I thought Roger would be the perfect husband. He was smart; he was well educated; he had good prospects."

"He took you in, Carrie, but you must realize that he took a lot of other people in too. This Mr. Hempstead, your boss, trusted him. And surely he was no fool."

"I'd have horsewhipped him if I'd known," Sam bellowed, when they told him what had happened. "A man who would lead an innocent girl on like that, while all the time he was stealing from an employer who trusted him. Yes, horsewhipped."

"Roger's being punished, Papa. When I saw him in court I only pitied him. I don't think he intended me any harm. He may even have loved me, in his way, just as he loved his mother. That's how it started, you know. He wanted money to make things easy for his mother."

"You're right enough about her." Sam stalked the kitchen, hands clasped behind his back. "She's as bad as he is, spreading all those lies about you after he said right out in court that you weren't in on his scheme."

"But Papa, it's all over now. And, though I never thought I'd admit it, some good things have come out of it."

"Sure. You're rid of the bum. It would have been much worse if he'd not been caught until after you were married."

"I don't mean just that, Papa, though it's true enough. But I've learned some important lessons. I've learned that I can't depend on appearances or respectability or money. I've learned that when it comes right down to it, the only things that can be relied on are the things we can't see with our eyes or hear with our ears. The only things that don't fail are those things I used to laugh at, things like love and dreams and faith."

"I know it's been terrible for you, Carrie, but the Lord has brought you back to us." Anna's plump arm circled Carrie's shoulders. "We're so happy for that."

"I really can't stay here indefinitely, though," Carrie reminded them. "There isn't room, and besides, I have to earn my own way."

"For now, we need you, Carrie." Anna settled heavily into the rocker. "You're the answer to my prayer. And after the baby comes, who knows what may happen."

"As Betsy said, people in San Francisco may have forgotten by then, or the Salvation Army people might be able to help me get another chance to salvage my reputation."

"Salinas City's growing," Anna suggested. "You might find work with your typewriting there, and you'd be closer."

Sam looked strangely at Anna as she spoke. "That's months ahead anyhow," he insisted. "Lots can happen before that."

Sunday morning dawned bright and sunny. Anna had enlisted in the Salvation Army, partly to please Sam, so Carrie's pale green suit with its fashionable bustle and full skirt contrasted with their dark uniforms as they sat together at the service. Carrie scanned the handful of worshipers, hoping to spot Matt.

Her newfound faith hadn't been strong enough to convince her he would be here, but he was. He was wearing the store-bought suit he'd worn for Sam and Anna's wedding, and it still looked stiff and strange on his stocky frame. His copper mustache had been neatly trimmed, and his cowlick was plastered down. Carrie smiled, knowing it would pop upright any moment.

Carrie's palms grew wet; her cheeks burned; her eyes filled with tears. The service began, and she tried to concentrate on the singing and the message, for she sincerely desired to serve the Lord with all her heart now. But that heart still ached for the fiery dreamer she'd fled a year and a half before.

After the last hymn had been sung and the altar call given, the McLeans filed out with the others. As Sam helped Anna down the steps, Carrie suddenly found herself facing Matt. She sought his eyes, but he evaded hers as if he were afraid of what he might see with that penetrating, knowing look.

215

"Hello, Carrie. I heard you'd come home."

"Yes, the first of the week." Her own words startled her. She was trembling so much she was surprised she could speak at all. Suppose he hadn't waited? It had been over a year. Suppose there was someone else? She forced herself to keep her reply impersonal. "I came back to help Anna."

"Oh, yes, I see." He nodded. "Morning, Sam, Anna. How's things?"

"Fine, just fine, Matt. And you?"

"Oh, great, Sam." He shifted his weight from foot to foot, and Carrie knew that he was as uncertain as she, for a change. "Workin' hard." He turned back to Carrie. "I'm still drilling wells, Carrie. Some new people are settling on the Fort Romie land, and we're putting in some good deep wells for them."

"The crops look very good this year." She struggled to make small talk, hoping no one else could hear the thumping of her heart. "I'm surprised people are drilling wells now, while the river's still full."

"Memories are short, but not that short. People have a little money now, and good contracts for their beet harvest coming up, but the drought's not that long past."

"Matt's been doing a good selling job," Sam boasted. "People hereabouts trust him."

Anna tugged her husband's sleeve gently. "Sam, I'm a bit tired. Could we get on home now?"

"Of course, Anna. See you later, Matt. Carrie, you coming?"

216

She started to follow, but Matt's eyes at last found hers. "Carrie, I'd like to walk you home, if you don't mind."

If she didn't mind! It would have broken her heart if he hadn't asked. "I'll be along in a few minutes, Papa."

Matt offered his arm then, and she took it as they strolled down the lane behind the scattering flock. "Carrie, Anna told me you were going to be married." He shortened his steps to match hers. "I'm sorry things didn't work out as you hoped."

"I'm not."

He didn't seem to hear. "I knew how much you wanted nice things and security." He turned down a narrow lane edged with willow saplings. "A little short-cut," he explained.

The lane led to the abandoned Andersen cabin, and Carrie knew it was no shortcut, but she followed anyhow. A few yards up the lane Matt turned to her. "Carrie, did you love him?"

The cowlick had erupted. His eyes met hers, but if he saw the answer he didn't trust it. "Carrie, maybe it's none of my business, but I have to know. Did you love him?"

"No, Matt."

"You promised to marry him."

"I liked him, or thought I did," Carrie admitted. "He was good to me. He promised me the kind of life I thought I wanted. But I didn't love him, ever."

"Is that why you didn't marry him?"

Why did Matt have to be so direct? "Not entirely. He . . ." No, Carrie wasn't ready to tell Matt the whole story yet. "He did something I couldn't forgive."

"Carrie, could you have married a man you didn't love, just because he offered you the kind of life you wanted?"

"The life I *thought* I wanted, Matt. I know now that I was wrong."

"Would you have gone through with it, married him, if nothing had happened to stop you?"

"Matt." Carrie reached out to him, but he didn't take her hands. "Matt, I can't lie to you. I might have. I don't know," she admitted. "But I know I'm glad I didn't. And I know that now I will never marry a man I don't love."

He took one hand and led her up the lane. As they drew near the cluster of mature willows that shaded the cabin, Carrie gasped. "Who lives here now, Matt? It's lovely."

An ell had been added to the kitchen side of the little cabin. It had been painted a warm cream color, and chocolate brown shutters framed the sparkling new windows. Snowy alyssum cascaded from a window box, and a transplanted wild rose twined through a new and intricately turned porch rail.

Matt led Carrie to the door, opened it, and gently pushed her inside. The old kitchen was now a neat, if nearly empty, parlor. Green and white wallpaper covered the rough planks, and a green and brown braided rug lay on the scrubbed and polished floor.

But Matt wasn't content to let her admire the parlor. He led her into the new ell. A wood stove filled the far end. A small oak table and two chairs stood in front of the window. A massive kitchen cupboard faced them, and next to it, on the wall, hung a galvanized iron sink. Matt

218

was like a schoolboy with a new toy he couldn't wait to show off. In one giant step he was in front of the sink, turning the porcelain handles above it.

As the clear, pure water flowed into the sink, he pulled her toward it. "Feel that, Carrie. Just feel it. Good, cool water. And all we'll ever need, from our own well."

"You believed, Matt. You kept believing. All the time I was struggling to make my fortune in the city, you kept believing."

"I did leave, Carrie, right after you did." His voice dropped. "Didn't see much point in staying around. But after I saved up some money I heard about the Army's change of plan."

"You mean their decision to resell the farms to farmers?"

"That's right, Carrie. When I heard that, I knew I'd been right about the Lord having a farm for me."

"And you came back, bought this place, and . . ." Carrie looked around the cozy house in amazement. "Look what you've done with it. It's beautiful."

"I knew you'd be back, Carrie," he said.

"But I was engaged to another man."

"At first," he shrugged. "But then Anna told me you had broken the engagement. That's when I really went to work on the place. On the house anyhow. I just knew you would come back home."

"I think I knew, too, deep down, when I decided to come home, that you'd be here waiting. And you promised me a house, Matt, but such a lovely house . . ."

"But it's going to be nicer, Carrie. We'll build on another bedroom or two and an indoor bathroom, too, one day."

219

Carrie laughed. "Matt, you've won. You don't have to make any more promises."

He gathered her gently into his arms, and his mouth found hers. There was no need to hurry. They had the rest of their lives to be together. But at last their bodies parted, for the moment.

They sat on the kitchen chairs and held hands across the table. "Carrie, I did it all for you—the house, the farm. You will share it with me, won't you? You will make all my dreams come true, won't you?"

"Yes, Matt, I will."

"And you're not marrying me just for my fortune?"

He almost seemed to be teasing her once more, but she knew he needed the answer.

"I told you I'd never promise myself to another man I didn't love, Matt. I won't marry you even for this beautiful home. But I will marry you, Matt Hanlon. Because I love you."

About the Author

Jean Grant was born in Michigan but has lived most of her life in northern California. She earned her bachelor's degree from the University of California at Berkeley, and has worked for more than thirty years as a clinical laboratory technologist.

Grant's first novel was The Revelation. Her articles and short stories have appeared in such publications as Evangelical Beacon, Mature Living, Home Life, Seek, and Power for Living.

Continue to share the story of Carrie and Matt with

Book Two
of the Salinas Valley Saga

The Promise of Peace

❧

Coming in January 1995